COLD BURN

AN IRON TORNADOES MC ROMANCE

OLIVIA RIGAL

Cold Burn
An Iron Tornadoes MC Romance

My name is Brian Hatcher and I want it all.

I want the control of the motorcycle club my father runs, the murderer of my friend David six feet under, and, more than anything, David's sister Lisa.

I want Lisa on the back of my bike, in my bed, and under the spell of my cold burn.

I don't care that Lisa's unsure of the role the Iron Tornadoes played in David's death or that her long-held goal is to become a criminal prosecutor.

I won't let her wishes stand in my way.

In the end I always get what I want.

SPECIAL THANKS TO

Christa Wick
& Zirconia Publishing
who helped me start this Wild Ride.

Cover by Jacqueline Sweet

Become a VIP Reader :
https://oliviarigal.com/VIP_BM_E

Everest is early. It's nine o'clock at night, and The Styx doesn't open before ten on Fridays.

"How are you doing, brother?" I ask as he enters the small room that serves as my office since I've become the manager of this MC sex club. I stand up, and we hug. Whoever came up with his nickname had a stroke of genius. Everest is indeed built like an impressive mountain. He even makes me feel small, and I'm anything but a miniature.

"Better than you," he says, looking very serious. "Seriously, Brian, you look like shit."

"Yep, and I feel worse than I look. That's why I asked you to come over tonight. Sledge is out of commission, and Mirror is away. Our crew is good for watching over the video feeds, and the bouncers are ready to intervene. But just in case something tricky happens, we need a Dom with brains and muscle. I'm too tired to play referee tonight."

"Yeah, yeah." He shrugs. "I'm not working before Monday anyway. Since they pulled me out of the task force, my schedule's been pretty relaxed."

"Why don't you quit and come work with us?" I ask out of force of habit as we walk toward the locker room.

We've had this conversation a thousand times already, but for some strange reason, despite having lost all his illusions about the force, he holds on to his police job. Obviously, he isn't there for the money. If he only worked here as Dungeon Master every third weekend and carried out a few missions a month for our Friendly Persuasion Agency, he could double his income.

"You're wasting your skills with those two-bit assignments they give you. With your talent for reading people, you're just what we need—"

"Save your breath," he says, interrupting my sales pitch. "Just know that lately, I've been giving it some serious thought, and I think you're right. It's about time I come into the family business."

I'm so surprised by his answer that I'm suddenly at a loss for words. He laughs—at the expression on my face, I guess—and he takes advantage of the situation to add, "Now that Cracker is thinking about stepping down, we'll both need someone to have our backs, and I can't think of anyone better suited to do that than a real brother."

"You're right." As I give him the answer he wants to hear, the face of another brother comes to my mind. David used to have my back, too. Through childhood, high school, and our Army years, I knew I could count on him. Always. I wonder if I'll ever be as close to Everest as I was to David. I miss his sorry ass and his wicked sense of humor.

"Thinking about David again?" Everest asks, looking a bit sad.

That man is perceptive. Sometimes he's so right on the money, it's scary. Not that I have anything to hide from him, but still, it's unsettling to be an open book, even to a trusted brother.

"Would you please get out of my mind and close the door behind you," I tell him as I playfully punch his shoulder. I laugh, but he doesn't even smile. I guess I need to explain. "He's on my mind because I got a postcard from him today."

"You what?" Everest almost shouts, stopping in his tracks.

"We had this joke that the first one who kicked the bucket would send a message to the other," I explain as I open my locker to retrieve my helmet and backpack. "Funny how I was kind of expecting it, and yet, it was a shock to get his postmortem card."

"I'm sure." Everest looks at me thoughtfully.

"I figure that at some point, probably before a crappy mission when we were in the service, he must have given the card to someone to send me for the anniversary of his death."

"Has it been a year already?" Everest frowns, probably trying to remember the date of David's death.

"Not yet," I say.

"I see. So what did he write?"

"That hell was just like Florida. Hot, humid, crowded, and infested with mosquitoes." I pause, and since Everest can read my mind anyway, I think aloud, "I wonder to whom he gave the postcard."

"Where was it sent to?"

"The Tornadoes clubhouse."

Everest raises a questioning eyebrow as he opens his own locker to change into his leathers. I consider the choice of mailing address and shrug.

"It makes sense," I say. "The only other stable address I ever had was my mother's house, and sending it there was not an option. She would have recognized David's handwriting and freaked. The clubhouse was a logical choice."

"Maybe you're right." Everest's tone doesn't match his words.

"Spit it out, bro. What's eating you?" I ask.

"I can't help thinking there's something fishy about David's death."

"What do you mean?" This is the first I've heard about this.

"First, there's the fact that his case should have been given top priority." He plops onto the bench to remove his riding boots. "The unspoken rule is that a cop's death never goes unpunished. It sends the wrong message to the perps, and it's bad for morale. So yeah, normally, there's almost no limit to the number of man hours spent on that type of case. No one stops until it's solved."

"And they didn't do that for David's case?"

"No. The top brass let it go cold, and no one except me seems to give a damn. Hell, even the captain, who's now married to David's mother, doesn't seem to care. So that started me thinking, and I asked around. You know what? No one has seen the corpse. I asked the captain, and no, Steven didn't see the body. He just took the medical examiner's word for it and took for granted what was in the report… David had been too badly beaten for an open coffin."

He stops talking as he removes his T-shirt and stretches to drop his boots on the bottom shelf of the locker. He must have been seriously hitting the gym lately because he's fitter than ever. A moving mountain of muscle.

"I thought that was weird, so I went to talk to our ME, and guess what? He didn't see David's body, either. The examination was carried out somewhere up north, in Okeechobee or Indian River—I can't remember."

"That makes sense. David's body was found north of Palm Beach County. The ME offices are probably territorial about the bodies found in their jurisdiction."

Everest nods to concede that point, but he continues, "Since there were no pictures in the file, I reached out and got zilch. Nothing—no picture of the crime scene, no picture of the corpse, no investigator notes. Not a thing. When I first called, I was told to put in the request through official channels. I did and waited, and when nothing came after a month, I called back. That's when I was told that the file had been misplaced."

I shrug. "That's not that unusual. Shit does happen. Files get lost. It shouldn't, but it does happen, even in the best run places."

"So I went to the funeral home and spoke with the manager. The man never saw David's body either. He got a sealed body bag from the ME and put it in the box that Lisa had picked without asking questions."

"And you kept this to yourself until today?" I ask, trying to hide my feelings from my voice. I'm not sure what those feelings are anyway, a mixture of anger and surprise, but mostly a sense of betrayal.

"Hell, yes! I didn't see the use in getting your hopes up. I know how close you two were. How old were you when your mother married his uncle Tony and you moved in next door to him? Five or six? He's been in your life forever, and I didn't see the point of cracking that door open in your mind if my suspicions were without merits. Today, this postcard sent to the clubhouse at your attention is the final nail… out of the proverbial coffin, so to speak."

I can't help but smile at his reverse image. Who else would pull nails out of the coffin? And he's right—since he's cracked the door open, I can't help but wonder. Now I have to get back into my room to look at the postcard again, to see if I missed a hidden message between the lines.

≈

2

I'm exhausted, but I won't fall asleep during the short ride between The Styx and the clubhouse. The conversation I just had with Everest jolted me awake, that and the rain that is starting to fall.

My mind travels back to the week before I left the academy. The placement office was setting up interviews for Internal Affairs and task force units. Could David have been recruited by two departments? It's possible that IA thought the biker task force unit needed investigating. And it sure did. Could things have gone so wrong that the department had to pull him out and fake his death?

Some days, I wonder how far IA can go to blur the lines. I'm not sure the police should be allowed to do that. Their excuse is that life isn't black and white, and they exist in the acceptable shade of gray. Hell, I should understand the need for the gray area—I live in that color spectrum.

As I park in the new barn of the clubhouse compound, the rain intensifies. The rainy season is early this year. I run from the barn to the main house. Living in the world capital of lighting-strike deaths is a major downside for bikers in Florida.

I step into a smoked-filled room, where my father is holding court, telling some story about his good old days, when he was Pain's sergeant at arms. His large gestures emphasize his every word. As if any story about the club founder needs emphasis. The man was the most fucked-up sadist I've ever met. Compared to him, my father's just a little twisted, and the kinkiest members of The Styx are regular choirboys.

He runs a hand over his shiny shaved skull. He started shaving it last year, when it began to fall out because of the chemo. He always had such a lot of hair, and seeing him without any is strange.

He looks in my direction, nods slightly, and goes back to studying the faces of his audience. He's such a good storyteller; everyone seems mesmerized, especially two young girls sitting next to him. If hearing about Pain, the founder of the MC, doesn't freak them out, they're seriously messed up, and that's just the way he likes them. Maybe we'll have a pair of extra sweet butts in house soon. If there's one thing to admire about the man, it's his stamina. I hope I'm still that green when I'm his age.

I climb the stairs to my room and grab the postcard I tucked in the side of the frame of the mirror above my dresser when I left this morning. I read David's familiar script.

"Sure feels like I'm still in Florida. It's hot, humid,

crowded, and infested with mosquitoes. I expect you to take care of Lisa, and I plan to come back to haunt you soon to check out you're doing it right. Take care, Bro."

I read those lines, looking for a coded message, but I see none. I'm not even sure why he underlined the word right. I understand it as a green light for my taking care of his sister the way I want to, but that's because it is what I want to read into it.

As far as I can tell, there are no hidden messages in this text. Nothing dates it. It could have been written five years ago or last week. I flip the card over and look at the picture. It's one of those typical Floridian views taken from a plane or chopper flying over the beach. There's a bit of water on the right, surrounded by the beach and oceanfront properties under a clear blue sky. In a sunny-gold fancy font, the beach is identified as Point Lookout, Florida. There are so many people on the beach that I suspect the photo was taken during a spring break party. All spring break beach parties look the same.

I curse Everest for getting my hopes up then drop the postcard on the dresser and get ready for a shower. I'm no longer mad at him; I understand why he kept his thoughts to himself. Like he said, it's going to be painful to close that door he cracked open in my head. I would never have shared such doubts with Lisa, so I can't blame him for keeping silent.

I sigh. David's really dead.

When I come out of the shower a few minutes later, my father is sitting on my bed, waiting for me. "Ice, you look like crap," he says.

"Thanks, I know. Everest just told me."

"There's shit we need to talk about. Tomorrow. My office. Noon."

When he's not trying to seduce an audience, my father is a man of very few words. Short sentences, no verbs if they're dispensable. He sounds like his favorite toy, the whip. He loves to crack it figuratively and literally. His affinity for it is probably the reason his friends call him Cracker. Plus, he's a proud Floridian. The name "Cracker" matches every aspect of his personality.

"Sure thing," I say. I'm relieved he doesn't want to talk now because I'm dead on my feet.

As he steps toward the door, his eyes fall to the postcard. He picks it up and stares at the picture for a few seconds before dropping it back onto the dresser. As he walks out, he says, "I know it was the right choice for the town, but this hotel sticks out like a sore thumb in the middle of Point Lookout. Night, Ice."

I throw the towel on the bathroom floor and crawl into bed. Surprisingly, I don't fall asleep as soon as my head hits the pillow. I haven't had more than five hours of sleep a night all week. I rode hundreds of miles to find a runaway kid and bring him back home to his parents. Why am I not sleeping?

Something's nagging me, but I don't know what. I'm not sure if it's something Cracker said or the fact that, for an hour, I hoped David wasn't dead. I toss and stare at the ceiling.

Lisa will be back soon. Just thinking of her gets me hard enough to pound nails. I close my eyes and remember how thoroughly sated she looked the last time I saw her. To make sure none of those fancy intellectual law school students caught her eye, I had been relentless with her. I made her scream my name all night long.

Just the thought that someone else could lay a hand on her gets me in full caveman mode. No sharing, not even with a brother. When Everest told me that he really liked her and that she had kissed him, it took all my willpower not to hit him. I probably would have punched anyone else.

She's mine. Fuck, she's always been mine, and that's just the way it should be.

Everest makes fun of me. He says it's the other way around, that I'm hers. He may have a point.

Except when I was acting as dungeon master and required to care for a poorly treated sub, I haven't touched a woman since she left. I wasn't even tempted. Nothing's wrong with the sweet butts in the club. Some of them are actually pretty hot, but my mind's not in that game anymore. No more mindless sex. I want the real thing, and the real thing is Lisa.

I flip onto my stomach and sigh in relief at the thought that my sexual dry spell is about to end. I think about the five acres of land I've purchased behind the clubhouse. It's ideal. There's a small lake and some beautiful trees. I could build her dream house on it. I would let her pick the layout, the builder—anything she damn well wants in every single room of the house, except for one.

I want one extra room in the house, one room that Lisa doesn't yet know we need to make our house perfect.

Our home will have a nice soundproof playroom for the two of us. A place where she can wail my name all night without waking up our children because there's no way in hell I'm ever taking her to The Styx.

3

"'B out time," my father says as I enter his office five minutes after noon. He looks exasperated, as if I were an hour late. He's forgotten that when I came in here ten minutes ago, he was on the phone and ordered me to leave.

His short-term memory is shot. That's the reason he's stepping down. Every so often, he has a lucid moment and realizes that his temper and a failing brain are a lethal combination that could put the club in danger. And the club is the only thing he's ever loved.

Cracker might also love Everest's mother, or so Everest thinks. I have my doubts, but then again, Everest's mother clearly satisfies a need that Cracker has. He stayed around for a couple of decades and still visits her and their daughter, whom he worships.

In Cracker's head, the lines between all forms of desire are blurred. Cracker's English resembles Spanish, in that it has only one word for the ideas of both wanting and loving. Still, Everest is probably right. Cracker still loves/wants his old lady.

And he does adore Juliya. Most of the time, I feel sorry for my sister. I can't imagine being the center of the old man's attention is easy. Plus, Everest and I are two overprotective brothers with an attitude. It must be a heavy weight to carry.

Juliya and the MC are all Everest and I share with Cracker, all we hold dearly enough to put up with him.

Cracker stares at a pad on his desk and frowns while going down the list he's written in large block letters.

"Xander Wild tour?" he asks.

"Yes," I say. "We're on. I'm taking four guys with me."

"Fine. How long will you be gone?"

"Just one week. We're only handling his security on the East Coast. We hand him over to another chapter as soon as he starts going west. You've got the schedule, and in case you have questions, Patricia will always know where to find us. After that, I plan to stay put for a couple of months."

Cracker frowns at the sound of my assistant's name. Patricia's not afraid of him. Hell, Patricia's not afraid of anyone or anything. She's the only dominant woman at The Styx, and Cracker is spooked by the very concept of a woman holding a whip. He has a hard time wrapping his mind around the fact that some straight men like being bottoms.

"We'll need to organize a meet with your brother when you come back." His eyes remain riveted to the pad.

"I need to decide to whom I'm going to be handing the gavel."

He can't seem to make up his mind which of his sons he wants to step into his shoes. He's told me he would favor Everest because he's been raised in the club, and he would have a firmer hand, which Cracker feels the club needs.

Cracker's right about Everest being tougher. No matter how much he denies it, Everest is just like our old man, bossy and manipulative. The major difference is that Everest's so smooth his victims don't realize they've been screwed until they're done for. He would indeed make the most effective president.

But as long as Everest doesn't walk away from his police job, it's not going to happen. His membership in the club is already very questionable. We're not an outlaw MC, per se. Most of the club's activities are legit, but close enough to borderline to draw the attention of Internal Affairs. So, for as long as he remains on the force, Everest will not be our prez.

"How are you feeling?" I ask Cracker.

"About the same way that you fucking looked yesterday," he growls. "Frustrated and way too tired for a man of my age."

"Anything I can do for you?"

"Yeah, talk your brother into coming here full time," he snaps back.

The man doesn't realize he should be more careful about what he wishes for. He's got no idea how lucky he's been that I am the only one he's had to deal with so far. Sure,

Everest and I are in agreement about the future of the MC. However, we have very different ideas about how to make that future happen. I think it best to let things take their natural course. I'm fine remaining the VP until Cracker steps down. Everest is not as patient. If he comes here full time, he'll not only do everything in his power to become president, he'll also make sure it happens right away.

But then again, Cracker may know that already. That could explain why he's tried to play us against each other. He failed. There will be no sibling rivalry on that front.

The same doesn't hold true as far as Lisa is concerned. I don't care what Everest thinks or feels. She's mine. Just mine. And when I see her next, she and I will have an interesting conversation about her going around kissing other men.

"Am I boring you?" Cracker barks.

"Sorry, Prez," I say. "I was distracted. What is it you were saying?"

"Juliya. She's coming home from college at the end of the spring term. She's gonna spend the summer at her mother's. She called to ask if you'd all be around, and she asked about the Fourth of July party." He looks at me with raised eyebrows.

"Yeah, yeah, I'll be here." Yep, his short-term memory is shot. I just told him two minutes ago that I was not going anywhere after my rock-star-sitting gig.

Even though I've totally taken over the management of two of the MC's activities I initially assisted him with, I go through the motions and spend the next half hour trying to bring him up to speed. It's useless, despite the notes he takes. He'll have forgotten all about it in a few hours.

We have nothing much to say about the activity of The Styx. In a sex club, when there's no drama, it's same old, same old most of the time.

I have tons to say, however, about the Friendly Persuasion Agency's booming business. Lately, we've been getting unofficial referrals from the police about cases in which their hands were tied. We're more efficient at times because we have no trouble crossing some lines the cops aren't even allowed to step on.

Also, unlike them, we're not hindered by state borders. That's the reason the police suggested the families go to us for help searching for their kids who had joined a new cult. We checked out the pseudo-religious association —a "church" that teaches "divine intervention through love"—that had come recruiting in our neck of the woods. It was just a front for a bastard to get his hands on fresh flesh and easy money.

After we brought back a few kids, the parents got together and hired us to invite the guru to move out of the state. After a little Friendly Persuasion Agency magic, he moved away. But he had his hooks deep in one of the kids. We brought him back home, but he was so brainwashed that he followed his mentor—and took a shitload of cash from his parent's home. I don't know what kind of business Carlos Sanchez's father is in, but if he had that much cash lying around, it couldn't be legit.

It took me a few days to find the conniving little brat. He fought me with so much conviction that I had to call in a cage to bring him home.

"How old is the kid?" Cracker asks after I tell him about Carlos.

"He'll be eighteen soon. Why?"

"Because he sounds like the kind of kid who's in bad need of guidance while we need new prospects," he answers with a smirk.

It never crossed my mind, but he's got a point. The kid's smart and lost. He needs to belong to something, and hanging out with us could help him get a better grip on life.

"You wanna take on another prospect?" I ask. "I thought we had all we needed, prospect wise"

"Naw, one of them quit last night after I demonstrated some whip techniques on one of the new girls." An alarmed look must have crossed my face because he adds, "Got no complaints from her. She's still in my bed, and I think she likes it there."

I shrug. "Fine, then I'll reach out to the kid when I come back."

We go over some more stuff before it's time for me to get ready for my next gig. Star-sitting should be interesting, especially since I do like Xander Wild's music.

$\sim$

4

The ride up from Point Lookout to New York State is uneventful. I picked Lobster and Waxer. They're probably not the sharpest of our club, but they're real tight and loyal to me. We're riding with a prospect whose name I can't seem to remember and an older member called Brains. He's not as quick on his feet in case we need to fight, but he's got street smarts. The four of us have worked together before, and we make a good team. I'm hoping some of our experience will wash over onto the prospect.

The first concert is set in Jones Beach Theater. As we drive east on the Meadowbrook State Parkway, I notice an exit sign for another Point Lookout. A home away from home. I wonder how many towns across the US share that name.

Even though it's early when we arrive, a big crowd has already gathered. I look at the faces as we slowly drive to the parking area. It's mainly kids, all looking dazed. They don't look stoned, but more like they need a nap, probably because of the sun. This is one of the first warm weekends of spring, and it's easy to get drunk on intense light exposure. Since Xander Wild's audience doesn't look dangerous, I wonder why he's hired us.

I checked him out before we left. Alexander Hughes, aka Xander Wild, is in his early thirties, just a few years older than I am. In his interviews, he says he has two daughters, but he's never been married, and no one has ever been able to identify the mother or the kids. His only family I could find is a brother, Andrew Hughes, who is a police officer in Manhattan. The only dirt I could dig up was Xander's reputation as a womanizer. No history of drugs or alcohol abuse. He's pretty healthy and balanced for a rock star.

His brother is the one who greets us at the gate that leads to the backstage area. Actually, "backstage" is not an appropriate term for the place since the back of the stage is against the ocean. Andrew Hughes isn't in uniform, but his badge is visible on his belt, and I can see he's carrying. His holster shows when he extends his arm to shake our hands. He introduces himself as Andy and directs us to a sheltered place where we park our rides next to two very customized Harley Davidsons.

"That one's mine, and the other one is Xander's," Andy says with obvious pride. "I escorted him outside of the city earlier, and it was a smooth ride."

"Any special reason why he hired us? Does your brother expect trouble?" I ask. "The crowd seems to be pretty tame."

"It's not the audience we're concerned about," Andy says. "It's retaliation from an angry family."

"What do you mean?" I curse myself for not following up on Patricia's booking of this gig. Maybe it's more than star-sitting.

"Well, there was this girl, a regular groupie. A glittery bag of bones who attended all of Xander's concerts in Manhattan last week. She managed to get banged by every member of the band, except Xander. He was not interested. He likes healthy-looking fleshy women." As he says this, Andy's hands go down in curvy motions, drawing a bomb-shell silhouette in the air. "Xander was so not into her that he couldn't even go for a pity fuck. The stupid MC princess was insulted, and she's told her father that Xander raped her."

"Oh, fuck," Lobster says. "What's the name of the MC?"

"It's a New York-based club, the Lady Liberty Bastards," Andy answers. "I checked them out. It's a small unit that has had very few brushes with the law. I don't think they're a once-percenters, but I'm pretty sure they won't let something like that slide."

"Did you try reaching out to them?" I ask.

"Hell, if the cunt's a tramp, everyone in the club must know it," Waxer says. For once, he's quick to stress a good point, but his vocabulary leaves a bit to be desired since he's speaking with a police officer.

"Maybe everyone but her father," Brains adds. "The dad and the husbands are always the last to know."

This is experience talking. The man's been married and divorced twice. He has three daughters with the first wife and two with the second. The last sweetie he brought with him to the club party is expecting. We all pray she delivers a son because six daughters are too much of a cross to bear for any man.

"Is there a phone I could use somewhere?" Brains asks. "I know a guy in that club. I'll try to reach out directly and see if we can't patch things up."

Before leaving the prospect with the bikes to keep watch, we each get our favorite weapon out of our saddlebags. I tuck mine, a brand-new Glock, into the back of my belt after putting a round in the chamber.

Andy accompanies us to the administrative facilities. He shows Brains into a small office and says he's going to give us a tour. But then he looks at his watch. "It's six already. I've got to leave you for half an hour. I have to pick up a gal at the train station in Long Beach."

"No sweat. We'll scout around, get our bearings," I say.

We explore the arena after he leaves. The crew is putting the finishing touches on the stage, and I recognize Xander Wild and several members of the band all the way in the back. I had never thought I would be able to identify them, but then again, their faces are on the record covers. I've listened to the man's records often enough to have looked at the cover hundreds of time and burn their faces in my memory.

As we get closer, Xander Wild frowns like someone wondering what the heck three random guys are doing on his set. Then he obviously remembers, because he walks in our direction and welcomes us.

"You must be the Friendly Persuasion protection unit." He extends his hand to me.

As he shakes everybody's hand, I make the introductions, "Lobster, Waxer, and I'm Ice."

"I'm pretty sure you've been called in for nothing," Xander says. "Yet I'm happy to see you, because you're going to make one old dream of mine come true. I'm going to do a short run with fellow bikers and make believe I'm member of an MC."

The man's smile is so sincere that the three of us smile right back at him. This is what charm is like. I thought my father had a lot, but this man oozes it. I take a step back to look around us as he lays it on for my two bros, who eat it up. I admire his ability. Not even a minute after meeting him, my men are so drawn in that they're treating him like a best friend they would do anything for.

If that's what he can do to those two, I can't imagine what his smile does to women and young girls. While he charms the others, I retreat to the back of the stage, where it drops into the ocean. The area is wide open, except for a little space hidden by three walls. It's an ideal hiding space, only a few steps away from access to the ocean. I walk to the edge, and, sure enough, steel bars jutting from the concrete make a rusty ladder perfect for using when arriving by boat. Crossing to the other side of the stage, I look at the arena and wonder how exhilarating it would feel to have thousands of people gathering to hear me sing.

Shaking my head, I try to look at my surroundings from another point of view. If I wanted to kill Xander, what would I do? I would wait until he got on stage because that's where he would be the most exposed. I place myself at the center of the stage and look for the place I would pick if I were a sniper hired to do that job. I slowly walk around the entire stage and notice another ladder, this one shiny and new, running up the wall of the concrete structure, all the way up to a platform, where the lighting equipment is set up. From there, I should get a better look at the place from a different perspective.

5

And a different perspective is what I really get as I look down on the stage. Andy's just returned with the woman he left to pick up at the station, and she's got that type of curvy figure that I love. If Xander likes his women with flesh on their bones, this one will be just about perfect. The man has good taste.

Xander waves at her, and I notice two things. Her left arm is in a sling, and as she gets closer to them, Lobster and Waxer get strange looks on their faces.

Xander picks up the girl cautiously and twirls her around him while she squeals with joy, "I can't believe I'm here!"

The man's got a goofy grin on his face as he asks, "And how's my favorite girl?"

That's when I see her face and blink. Twice. This can't be.

"She's great," the woman answers, and I know I'm

not hallucinating. This is Lisa's voice. What the fuck! She's his favorite girl now?

I hurry down the structure, praying that when I get back on stage, Xander will have put her down. If he hasn't, there will be no need to protect him from the Lady Liberty Bastards. I will have taken care of him myself before they have a chance to get to him.

As I take the last steps to the stage, my blood is pounding so loudly in my ears that I almost miss the rest of Lisa's answer.

"Alexandra's just fine," she says. "She's going to be so mad at me if she ever finds out I went to your concert without her, she'll…" Lisa stops in mid-sentence when I land back on stage.

She's midway between me and my guys. She seems to have recognized them, but she hasn't seen me yet. She steps away from Xander then takes another step back. Her voice is shaky as she asks, "What are those guys doing here?"

From behind, I can't see Xander's face, but I hear concern in his voice.

"Lisa, baby," he says. "There's nothing to be afraid of. They've been hired for my protection during the tour." He reaches a hand in her direction, but she recoils and keeps on walking backward, shaking her head, until she bumps into me.

She spins around to face the obstacle preventing her from retreating any farther, then she lifts her eyes to my face. It's her turn to blink. She raises her right hand and puts it on my chest as if to make sure that she's not dreaming. Her face softens.

The fright inspired by a chance encounter with two Iron Tornadoes on the stage turns into an expression of surprise. She's no longer afraid, but I can't tell if she's happy to see me or not.

"Brian," she whispers, and the way she says my name conjures images of her naked body under mine. I almost forget where we are. I want her so badly that I struggle to keep my composure. I want to drag her to a quiet corner behind the stage and do her standing up against the wall.

I take a deep breath and remember that right this second, it's not about me—it's about the MC. Forget about Brian. I'm Ice. I'm here for business. I have to be a coldhearted son of bitch who's in charge of protecting a client, not some idiot ruled by his dick. But when I'm done with business, I will need to teach her a lesson, because my girl can't be seen jumping in the arms of another man.

I don't care if he's a super-famous rock star. He could be the fucking president, and that wouldn't change a thing. She's mine, and she's got to remember that. So I don't smile at her. Instead, I grab her good arm and glare at Xander as I say, "If you want us to keep you safe, you need to let us restrict access to the stage."

Xander protests, "Lisa's no threat! She's family. She works for my ex."

Andy explains, "Yeah, she used to be Lyv's best waitress, but since she got mugged, she can't carry a tray. So Lyv's got her babysitting the kids."

My eyes jump from Xander to Lisa, and I see the yellowish skin on the arm she's got tucked in the sling. I refrain a gasp. Those are traces of serious bruising. I can't believe I didn't notice it right away. Shit. My girl's been hurt.

Fuck, I don't care what anybody else thinks. I release my grip from her good arm and wrap myself around her. I want to shield her from all the evil of the world.

"Oh, baby," I whisper in her ear. "I'm so sorry."

I feel her body mellowing against mine as she brings her good hand to my face.

"I'm fine now, Brian, really." Her eyes are shiny, like she's fighting tears. Her hand fists into my hair, and when she pulls my mouth to hers, it's like coming home. I lift her against me and devour her mouth. I want her so badly, I growl. For a time I can't measure, I get lost in her. Catcalls from my crew bring me back to reality. Brains, who just joined us, is the loudest.

"I take it those two know each other," Xander says.

Andy snorts. It shouldn't take a first-class detective to figure that one out.

"She's his sweetie," Waxer says. With a disgusted tone, he adds, "And he's really got it bad because he won't share, and he—"

"Shut the fuck up," I tell him. No need for Lisa to know that I've been a stupid monk ever since she's left.

I turn to Brains. "So what did you find out?"

"That we should be cool," Brains says. "The guy I knew let me speak to their VP. He told me their prez knows his daughter's a slut, so he probably won't want blood. But he'll want some show of good faith so the club can save face."

Brains turns to Xander and tells him about the offer he negotiated. "In the fall, they have this big rally for some charity. If you do the run with them, everyone comes out a winner. You get to ride with them—which should be cool—your presence gets them extra exposure for their cause, and you come out looking like a generous guy."

"Sure, sounds cool. I could do that," Xander says.

"They're voting on it tonight, and he'll let us know tomorrow."

"Fine work," I tell Brains. He's really good at this, and he gets how saving face is important.

"So I guess I won't be needing you guys after all," Xander says.

"Why don't we wait until tomorrow?" Brains says, and the caution in his voice leads me to believe he hasn't been totally forthcoming with the information he obtained.

"Right, let's wait until we get their word," I say. "I'll call the other charters later tonight to let them know you may be canceling before the end of the week, but we'll stick around for now."

The first week is nonrefundable anyway, and his production company already paid up front.

After checking with Lisa to see if she needs anything from him, Xander gets back to business. Lisa tells him she'll be fine and snakes her right arm around my waist. She smiles at me, and I feel about ten feet tall. Waxer's right. I've got it bad.

≈

6

After Xander leaves, Brains gives me a look and I step aside with him leaving Lisa under the watch of Andy and my two guys for a minute.

"The guy I know told me they have a loose cannon. The guy's called Crazy Eddy. Figures, right? He has the hots for the daughter of their prez, and my guy wouldn't put it past him to try something on his own to score points with the bitch."

"So we could have one man from their crew trying to score on his own tonight," I say. "I want two guys tagging Xander at all times up until the concert starts. This place is like a regular Swiss cheese. You can get in from every side, even from the ocean. Once the concert starts, we'll split around the stage. Right now, I'll go get the rest of the gear from the bikes," I tell him.

"I can do that," Brains says.

"Nah, I'm good," I tell him. Then I take Lisa with me

to go back to the prospect and the bikes. I don't let Brains go for the walkie-talkies because I have a special request for the prospect. I need his condoms.

"So you're a babysitter now," I say to Lisa as we walk back toward the parking area.

"Yeah, I was useless at the restaurant," Lisa explains. "I moved in with Lyv and her kids after her husband went AWOL and she realized she was expecting. I spent the end of the spring term with her. I saved rent, and she had help when she came home. At the end of the month, she's shipping the munchkins to the Hamptons for the summer, and I'll come home to prepare for the bar exam."

"We need to talk about your return," I say to her as we get to the lot. I tell her to take a seat on a bench for a few minutes while I talk to the prospect. My question makes him laugh. Of course he's got condoms. Who goes on a trip without a couple of fresh boxes? That's the question I can read in his eyes. Idiots like me, I guess. He gives me one box.

"Thanks, kid." I still can't remember his name. "I owe you."

He grins. What prospect doesn't want to be owed a favor from his VP?

He actually seems like a smart one because he didn't stay idle twirling his thumbs while we walked around. He's rechecked all the equipment and made sure the batteries were charged and all units were tuned to the same frequency. We're all set, and he's already got his earpiece in with the little receptor in the pocket of his cut.

I put mine on and shove a couple of condoms into

my back pocket. I give the rest of the box back to him then return to Lisa, who remained standing next to the bench. Of course, since I told her to sit, she had to stay up.

"Everything's all right?" she asks.

"Sure. Got to get these to the guys." I show her the bag with the rest of the transceivers. "And then we'll find a quiet place to talk," I tell her with a grin. Talking is the last thing on my mind. I need her so fucking bad, I want to find a place, like, right now. Until I make her mine again, I won't be able to think straight.

On the way back to the stage, I quickly run through the images in my head of my earlier reconnaissance of the arena. That's when I see it—the perfect hideaway for a hit man. It's at the back of the stage. It's sheltered on every side but the one facing the ocean. It's perfect for what I need.

I find Brains and Andy first. They're keeping a lookout on the front of the scene, watching the arena fill up. I give each one a device. Lisa and I walk to the sound control room, which is already a bit packed with the sound engineer, Xander, and two members of his band. My two guys, who would have overcrowded the place, are standing by the door. I give them the bag and get going with Lisa.

She stays as silent as I am, and this is starting to worry me. Lisa's a real chatterbox, except when she's pissed. She's got this infuriating habit of clamming up when she's upset. This used to drive David and me up the wall. We preferred a good screaming match to clear the air over this cold-shoulder treatment. When we were kids and she bottled up, we would tease her endlessly until she became so mad that she finally had to yell at us and tell us what was eating her up. It's her lucky day, because I'm in a teasing mood.

We reach the hidden corner I was thinking about when she starts talking.

"What are you smiling about?" she asks.

"Just thinking about what I'm going to do to you."

She rewards me with her magical smile.

Good, maybe she wasn't pissed after all.

I press her gently against the wall. "Do you know what I'm going to do to you now?"

She looks straight into my eyes and caresses my jawline with the back of her right hand. She stands on her toes to brush her lips against mine. Giving me a sweet, almost innocent, smile, she says, "I really have no clue. Why don't you enlighten me?"

I take her hand and raise it above her head, almost crushing the lower part of her body against the wall with my hips, and watch her pupils dilate. She's as turned on as I am.

"Baby, first I'm going to kiss you." My hand slides over her flesh until I'm palming her breast. "My fingers are going to explore every part of your body until you beg me to fuck you." I tweak the nipple hardening beneath my touch. "By the time the band starts to play, you'll be screaming so loud you won't be able to speak for a week."

"Is that so?" As I nod, she taunts me, "Bring it on, big guy. Give me your best, because there're very few things I'm sure about in life, but that's one. I will never beg."

And just like that she unleashes the monster in me. Poor baby, she has no clue she's just signed up for a serious cold burn. She's just about to find out why my crew calls me Ice.

~

7

I begin with her mouth. God, I've dreamed about it for way too long, and the small taste I had earlier on the stage just whetted my appetite. I nibble her lower lip then demand passage, which she does not deny. She opens for me, and I can feel that she's about as hungry for me as I am for her. She sucks me in and arches against the wall, pushing her hips against mine, grinding herself against me. And she thinks I won't get her to beg.

Her left arm in the sling is in the way, but I manage to slide my right hand under her shirt. I pull my mouth away to watch her face as my hand crawls up her side. I start with a gentle caress, but as I reach her breast and apply more pressure, her breath catches in her throat. Then she winces, and tears pool in her eyes.

Something's very wrong. This is a woman who can never get me to suck on her breast hard enough. I flip her around to make her face the wall, and I lift her shirt. The entire left side of her torso is the same shade as her arm. Someone gave her a serious beating, but only on half of her body.

I put my lips on her bruised shoulder. "Oh, baby, what happened?"

"I told you," she says. "I got mugged. At the beginning, it was awful. I'm much better now. Just be gentle when you touch that side."

"They did a number on you. Why didn't you just give them your bag?" I ask. "Whatever was in there sure wasn't worth getting killed over."

She turns to face me, lowering her shirt. "They didn't want my bag. They wanted my leather jacket. I couldn't let them have it—it was David's, and that's all I have left of him." She blinks furiously to keep the fresh tears in her eyes at bay.

"Tell me more. Did you see the face of the man who did this to you?" I'm feeling murderous. No one—absolutely no one—touches my girl and gets away with it.

"I was walking to the restaurant and about to cross the street." She shudders and closes her eyes as she remembers. "They were two guys on a Harley. Black leather. No patch. Full face helmet with shaded visor. The passenger, he grabbed the jacket, but I held on. He dragged me for an entire block."

"Did you notice anything special?" I ask.

"Not really. The only thing I could see was the guy's hand. Large. Very pale skin with spots. Larger than freckles. Probably a pigmentation disorder. On the top of the hand there was a tilted Swastika."

"What do you mean tilted?" I think I know what she means, but I need to make sure.

"I mean not the auspicious oriental symbol for eternity, but the tilted version that's the Nazi symbol." She opens her eyes and looks behind me, into the distance.

The backstage lights go off, and I can hear the first measures of Xander Wild's latest hit song.

My mind's already racing back home. A few months ago, Everest admitted that when David died, the task force they were both a part of was not investigating us. I was certain of that. No matter how much the brass trusted my brother, they would not have kept him in a unit that was investigating a club run by his own family.

Even though the brass kicked Everest out of the task force unit after David's death, Everest hasn't spilled the beans about his investigation. But once in passing, he did mention something about a white supremacy group and a local MC they would be working with. Could this be related?

The more I think about, the more far-fetched it seems. Even if David had indeed been hiding something in his jacket, I can't see how this all adds up to Lisa getting mugged that way. How would they have known about it? How would they have found out that Lisa took the jacket with her? How would they have figured out where to find her? But then again, trying to steal that jacket makes no sense unless they wanted something hidden in it. It's just a plain, worn black biker's jacket.

Anyway, I'm not letting her go back to New York for longer than it will take to pack her shit. She's coming home with me. I can't protect her if she's seven states away from me.

The loud bass changes rhythm, jolting me out of my train of thought. Xander Wild is best known for two things: sad lost love ballads and violent, angry rock songs. Tonight, he's starting slow.

Lisa closes her eyes again and sings along. "I never would have guessed how much I'd miss you…"

"I've missed you, too." I start kissing her again, keeping a little distance between our bodies for fear of hurting her. I sigh; my dry spell is not ending here. But it's still ending tonight. I plan to take her back to the hotel and keep her with me.

She slides her good hand under my shirt to pull me in, but when she reaches the center of my back, she lands on my gun. I feel her fingers tentatively touching the contour of the weapon before her hand withdraws. I catch it and thread our fingers together then lift her arm above her head.

I bury my face into the right side of her neck and breathe in her intoxicating smell. There's something flowery that's probably her perfume, then there's her own delicious smell. If I can't bang her against the wall, I can still make good on my promise to make her scream my name. The begging will have to wait for later or maybe even another day. Right now, I want to make her forget about her bruises and her pain. I want to be the center of her universe again.

"Brian," she says.

"Yes, sweetheart."

"I think I heard a noise outside," she tells me.

I stiffen. "What kind of noise?"

"Maybe the noise of a boat banging against the concrete," says a male voice at my back, and before I have any time to react, I feel something cold press against my neck—the round muzzle of a gun.

❧

8

"Now the position I have you in right now is a good start," the man says. "Do the same with your other arms and don't try anything stupid."

As I lift my second hand above my head, Lisa slides sideways from me. She moves her elbow slightly to make it more visible to the man behind me.

"My left arm is broken. Look, it's in a sling. There's no way I can lift it."

"Did that bastard do this?" the man growls. "Because if he did, I can take care of him for you."

Lisa shakes her head. In a very sweet voice that's so unlike her, I would laugh if I didn't have a gun to my neck, she says, "Oh, really. You would do that for me?" I can't see her face, but I'm pretty sure she's got a real Southern belle act going on, batting her eyelashes and all.

"Thank you, sir," she drawls. "It's nice to know there

are some real gentleman left in this uncivilized world. I've always thought the bikers are the modern-day knights."

"That we are, sweetheart," he answers with obvious pride in his voice.

"Well, sir, you don't need to hit him or anything, but if you could ask him to let go of my right arm, I would be most grateful."

"Sure thing. Hey, Tornado," he says, demonstrating that he can read my MC name on the back of my cut. "You heard her."

Without moving anything else so as to keep on sheltering most of Lisa's body, I let go of her right hand I had been pinning against the wall.

"Well, thank you," Lisa purrs, bringing her right hand down slowly. "What are you going to do with us now? Are you going to tie us together with our belts so you can go about your business without hurting us?"

While she speaks, she slides her right under my shirt. I feel her turn the switch of the walkie-talkie then reach for the gun at my back. She pulls it out of my belt and brings it next to her left arm. As I look down, I see she's hiding it in her sling.

"Yeah, I could do that," the guy says, his tone hesitant, as if he hadn't yet given any thought about what he was going to do next.

Fuck, it's amateur night. This is bad. I'd rather deal with a professional any day.

"So you came in by the sea?" Lisa asks. "That's so smart. No one thinks to watch for intruders on that side. I'm sure they're confident the proceeds of the show are safe in the side office."

"I'm not here for the money," the man protests.

"Then what are you here for?" Lisa asks, sounding genuinely curious.

"To do justice for my girl. No one messes with Eddy's girl," he growls.

So this is Crazy Eddy. Amateur and crazy. I'm watching Lisa playing with a live grenade, and I'm a sick bastard because I kind of think it's hot. I hope she can stall him until my crew gets over here.

"Oh, Eddy," she purrs. "Your girl is so lucky to have found a man like you."

"How do you know my name is Eddy?" he snaps at her.

"You just said, 'No one messes with Eddy's girl.' So I assumed it was your name," she explains, using a tone a very patient mother would take to speak to a temperamental child.

"Oh… right." He huffs.

The music stops for a moment, and the crowd cheers.

"I'll remove his belt now," Lisa says. "But with only one good hand, I won't be able to help you tie him up."

"Don't worry, sweetheart. I'll take care of it." The beginning of a new song almost drowns out the end of his sentence.

Lisa struggles to unhook the belt buckle with one hand then slides the belt through. The walkie-talkie falls to the ground and shatters. Crazy Eddy doesn't seem to notice. Xander Wild is singing something about a revolution, and the heavy metal sounds blasting around us cover everything else.

Lisa moves away from me and holds the belt toward Crazy Eddy.

"Hold it," he yells at her. Then he kicks the backs of my knees as he screams over the music, "Kneel. Hands behind your back."

While I drop to my knees, the muzzle of the gun ceases to be in direct contact with my neck, and I breathe a little easier. The man doesn't seem trigger happy, but still, he's dangerous because he doesn't seem to know what he's doing. Slowly, I do as he says and put my hands on the small of my back.

From the corner of my eye, I watch him take the belt from Lisa's hand. She takes a step backward so that her back is to the second wall of our little hideaway. I mentally order her to run past Eddy and onto the stage, but she doesn't do that. Instead, she calmly reaches into her sling and waits for him to put his gun into his belt. When he takes my belt with both his hands, she pulls out my gun and aims it at him.

Lucky for her, my gun is a Glock that's meant to be carried loaded. Otherwise, we'd be in deep shit. With just one hand, she couldn't have chambered a round.

"Eddy," she yells. "Drop your gun."

He jerks around in her direction and reaches for his gun. Before he has a chance to raise his arm, all hell breaks loose. I hear two shots, and Crazy Eddy goes down, cursing a blue streak. He falls onto my back, bringing me down, and he's no lightweight. As I struggle to get his body off me, I watch Lisa, with her back to the wall, slide to the floor as if she's in slow motion. "Don't be hurt. Don't be hurt. Please don't be hurt," I chant to myself.

Andy kneels by Lisa's side while Brains helps me stand.

"Are you all right?" he asks, and I can see the man truly cares for her. Before jealousy and fear have a chance to tear me up, I hear Lisa calling my name.

"I'm here, baby." I kneel beside her and cradle her face in my hands.

"Did I shoot you?" she asks, scanning me with her eyes.

"No, you just got the bad guy," Brains answers for me. "You're an excellent shot."

She shakes her head. "No, I'm not. We were lucky."

Andy laughs. "I've gotta hand it to you, Lisa, you do look at the bright side of life. You get mugged and then you get shot at, and you consider yourself lucky."

She smiles back at him. "Damn right, I'm lucky. I'm still here, and all I got is a bruise and a light shoulder wound. It's light, isn't it?"

Andy's raises his hand from her shoulder, and when he stops applying pressure to the top of her right arm, blood soaks her shirt. He presses down again, saying, "It doesn't look too bad, but we're going to have a doctor check it out."

"What about him?" Lisa points to Crazy Eddy with her chin.

"He'll live," Brains says. "But he may not walk or use his right arm for a while."

∾

9

I'm so wired that I can't sleep. I pace in my small hotel room while Lisa sleeps like a baby. When I brought her back last night, she was high on painkillers, so high that she couldn't stop talking about how scared she had been of losing me. She said that she didn't think she could have gone on with life if she lost me, too. I watched her fall asleep next to me, and the moment was so sweet, it was almost painful.

The ER nurse recommended a body pillow to help her find a comfortable position, so I made one for her with extra pillows I wrestled from the night manager. She's lying on her side, propped up on the pillows.

Now, as I watch her in the penumbra, I know what I should be doing. I should walk away from her. I should let her go find someone nice and safe, who would take her far, far away from me so that I never have to see her again.

But the very thought of never seeing her again rips me to shreds, and the idea that someone else would hold her and share her life is just unbearable. She's mine, and Everest is right on the money—she owns me. Shielding her body with mine yesterday didn't require any thought. I did it because it was the right thing to do. She owns my heart, she owns my soul, and she owns my body.

Is this why Cracker is a selfish and cruel bastard? Because he never got to find or keep someone who made him feel complete? I freeze that line of thought. It's easier to think he's just a sadistic bastard because that's his nature. I can't go around finding excuses for him. If I do, I'll start feeling sorry for the old man, and that would make me vulnerable. We only manage to work as a team because I've never shown him a weakness.

Would making Lisa my old lady be considered a weakness? I shrug. Probably. Cracker would think I'm caving in too early in the relationship. That option would make her safe from anyone in the club, and especially from Cracker. Each member's property is sacred.

But then Lisa is going to be a lawyer. Even if she didn't join the DA office as she always said she wanted to, there would be ethical issues.

Fuck, it would have been better if she'd decided to become a doctor or a nurse. We're always in need of medical attention, and having someone available for an emergency would be a blessing for the MC. But then medical professions have a code of ethics, too, and I think there are some wounds they need to report to the authorities…

"Hey," Lisa says, derailing my train of thought. "What are you doing up?" She starts to raise her right arm toward me to beckon me to her, but she quickly puts her arm down. I take one of the painkillers the doctors prescribed and a small bottle of water from the dresser and sit beside her on the bed. I help her sit up and make her swallow the pill.

"Come back to bed with me," she says. "I'm cold without you."

I slide behind her and pull the covers over us. She's warm and soft and so... right. Next to her is where I belong. She's my slice of heaven, and I'm never letting her go.

"As soon as the doctors say you're well enough to travel, I'm putting you on a plane or a train and taking you home," I tell her.

"Oh, crap," she says. "I need to call Lyv and tell her. I'm now totally useless, and she needs to get reorganized."

"Yes, she does. It's settled—you're coming home with me."

Lisa doesn't answer right away. She takes a breath as if she's going to say something, then she stops. I can't see her face, but I can almost hear the wheels of her brain churning. She wants to ask something but doesn't know how to put it.

I nuzzle the back of her neck and ask, "What is it? You should never be afraid to tell me anything. I want you to trust me, to trust me absolutely."

She sighs. "Where is home, Brian?"

Oh, right. I hadn't thought about that. I'm not sure living in the MC clubhouse is the best place for her, especially while she's preparing for the bar exam. If she stays with her mother, I'm not sure I'll be welcome, and we sure aren't going to camp on my piece of land. So I guess we need a rental while we build our own home.

"That's an easy question, baby," I whisper in her ear. "Home is anywhere I'm with you."

My answer seems to suit her because I feel her body relax, and she snuggles against me. Of course, now I have a boner that will never quit, and there's nothing I can do about it. Funny how it doesn't really matter. This is not just about her smoldering pussy, her delicious mouth, or her tasty skin; it's about all of Lisa. I don't need to be buried balls deep in her to know that she's my Lisa.

So I rest one arm on her waist and close my eyes. I'm never, ever letting her go.

10

A few hours later, Lyv comes to pick up Lisa at my hotel to drive her back into town. She steps out of the car and is about to hug Lisa when she slaps her forehead with her hand.

"Duh, I'm sure hugging you is not the smart thing to do," she says. Winking at Lisa, she turns to me. "I think I'll hug him instead."

Her hug is like a full-body wrap. She's just as soft and curvy as Lisa is, maybe a little more boobs and belly because her pregnancy is starting to show. They smell the same, probably the same shampoo or body soap. Even if they don't really look alike, there is a real kinship between the two. They're like soul sisters… and my body tells me that I could do Lisa's sister. My brain and my body have an argument, and my body wins. It's a healthy male body, which has been tempted all night after being deprived for so long. Clearly, it cannot not react to such softness.

When I found out she was pregnant, I knew she

couldn't be as old as I had initially imagined when Lisa first talked about her boss who owned several restaurants. Still, I didn't imagine her that young and yummy looking.

Xander Wild does have good taste.

"Nice to meet you," she says, looking at me straight in the eyes after she lets go of me. "I understand you're following us to the city?"

I watch Lisa slowly enter the car and hear the kids in the backseat welcoming her with shrieks of joy, or maybe of awe at the spectacular bandage she has on her right shoulder.

My gaze comes back to Lyv, and I nod. "Yeah, I want to help her pack her things, and—"

"Don't bullshit me." She drives an accusing finger into my chest. "I can pack for her. Tell me you want to spend more time with her. Tell me you want to check me out before you leave her in my care for a few days. Tell me you want to look at her leather jacket to figure out why someone tried to steal it from her, but do not bullshit me."

I laugh and plead guilty. "All of the above," I admit. "Plus, I heard that your food is spectacular, and I skipped dinner yesterday. I'm famished, and I'm also hoping to get a good meal. If you feed me, you'll make me a happy man."

She smiles, and she's even prettier. Not spectacularly good looking but warm and caring. Really lovely.

"As long as you make Lisa happy, you'll get all your wishes granted from me." She gets back behind the wheel, and I wonder why Xander Wild let her go. She's obviously a keeper. Just like Lisa, she's got the whole package. Curvy looks, smarts, and a positive attitude.

She gives me the address of a red-brick building on the corner of 57th and Third and tells me to park my bike in her underground garage, where the attendant will direct me to her parking spaces. She drives away, and I stay behind to check on my crew. I go knock on Brains's door. He's sharing the room with the prospect. He opens the door, and I can see they're all packed up and ready to go ride with Xander and Andy to the next venue later today.

"How did it go, bro?" Brains asks.

"Perfect," I say. "We should always have a cop witness our shootings. It really lightens up the questioning. Plus, Andy let them know that Lisa's brother had been a fellow officer who died on the job. It was smooth as silk."

"How badly was Crazy Eddy hit?" the prospect asks.

"He got one in the arm. It looked close range, so I think it's Lisa's handiwork. He got another one in the thigh," I tell him. "He'll probably limp, but he'll live."

"That's good," Brains says. "From what I gathered, he's not a bad guy. Just a misguided dick. An idiot, crazy in love with his prez' daughter."

Crazy Eddy's lucky Brains is getting soft with age. If I had been in his shoes, there would have been no question about my aim. When a man puts a gun to one of my brothers' heads, he signs his own death warrant. Maybe Brains's show of mercy will have earned us a favor with the Lady Liberty Bastards that we'll be able to cash in someday.

"Did you hear from Waxer and Lobster?"

Brains and the prospect laugh.

"Yeah, we heard them alright. Lucky I had Earplugs here with me," Brains says, pointing to the prospect. "Otherwise, we would never have slept."

The kid shrugs and explains. "I had to share a room with Lobster before…" He leaves us to fill in the rest.

I wink at Brains. "Looks like you may have picked a name for him."

"Earplugs?" The incredulous look in the kid's eyes is priceless. "You're gonna call me Earplugs?"

Brains tells him, "Sounds good to me. You can build a legend around it. Work on it, and it will help you score points with the chicks. Something like, 'I make them scream so loud that neighbors complained they had to get earplugs.'"

A smile starts to grow on Daniel's face. Sure, now that we've found a nickname for him, his real name comes to mind. The kid shakes his head and looks ready to embrace his new name.

"We'll give them a wake-up call around ten and meet with Xander and Andy at noon by Jones Beach," Brains tells me. "You're riding with us?"

"No, I've got something to finish up in Manhattan, and then I'll join you."

"Finishing up something?" Brains sneers. "That's what you kids are calling it now?"

The prospect snickers, and I glare at him. I give him my worst stare, the one that puts the subs in a catatonic state, and he lowers his gaze. I smirk. Who would have thought? He's built like a regular quarterback, and he's a sub. Whether the prospect gets his patch or not, I'm bringing him to The Styx when we get home. He's gonna be a perfect playmate for Patricia, my cute assistant who moonlights as a dominatrix.

I walk out to my bike and realize that there's another business I could start: a BDSM matchmaker agency. As I drive away, I try to come up with a good name for the place, something like Master Matching, Dungeon Dating… I'm truly certifiable!

11

B y the time I get to Lyv's place, I'm famished, and the smell of pizza hits me right in the gut. Lyv shows me the bathroom, where I wash my hands, and when I come out, I follow the sound of laughter to a large room that looks like it's a dining room, living room, and playroom all in one.

It's got a messy, homey feeling that makes me feel comfortable right away. Lisa's sitting at a large table with the kids, joking with them as they munch on pizza slices, and the last doubts I had about starting a family vanish in front of this domestic scene.

Yeah, she's the one I want behind me on my bike and in my bed for the rest of my life. I want to find her just like that, minus the wounds obviously—laughing with our kids when I come home.

Lyv sneaks up behind me, holding a fresh pizza pie. She stops next to me and stands on her tiptoes to whisper in my ear, "Lisa's great with kids. She's got the right combination of love and firmness."

Lisa looks up at me and smiles. "Here you are. We started without you. The kids were starving," she says. "Brian, these are my buddies, Alexandra, who's nine—"

"Nine and a half," Alexandra interjects.

"And Oliver, who is seven."

"Nice to meet you." I shake the hand that Oliver extends to me. I wouldn't want to offend the little man.

"Are you Lisa's boyfriend?" Alexandra asks.

"Alexandra!" Lyv scolds. "You know better than to ask personal questions."

She tries to look contrite but totally fails.

I wink at her and ask, "What do you think?"

She studies my face. "Yeah, I think you're the reason Uncle Andy's not getting anywhere with her."

Lisa laughs. "Andy's not interested in me, honey. He's been dating Mary Ann forever."

"Duh… it's been ten years, and they're still dating." Her little fingers do quotation marks around the word dating, and I realize that Alexandra does not look at life through the rose-colored glasses I thought the girls her age wore. How did she get so cynical at age nine… and a half?

"Yeah, Alexandra," I tell her. "You're right. Lisa and I go waaayyy back."

"I knew it. I knew it!" Alexandra yelps. "And will you—"

"Enough, young lady," Lyv says, and the little girl clams up.

Alexandra looks mainly like her mother, but I can see something of Xander Wild in her, somewhere in the shape of the eyes maybe, or just the eyebrows. Oliver doesn't look anything like either of them. He probably takes after a different father. He's quiet, but he doesn't seem to miss a thing.

We have a pleasant meal with the children, who quickly get excused from the table. Oliver's playing with a few cars and a fun-looking miniature garage while Alexandra curls up with a book on the sofa. I'm pretty sure she's not going to read a single word but eavesdrop on our conversation.

Lisa watches me observing Alexandra. "Does she remind you of someone?"

I nod as I remember Lisa doing the same when we were kids. David and I would run off while Lisa hung back then gave us a full report on the tidbits of interesting information she had gathered while listening in on the adults' conversation.

After serving us a fabulous tiramisu and a very strong Italian coffee, Lyv excuses us, as well. Sounding very motherly, she says, "You kids may go play in Lisa's room now, but don't make too much noise. Mommy will be taking a nap on the sofa."

She does indeed go lie down with her head next to her little girl's lap. Following Lisa across the room, I witness a strange role reversal as Alexandra tenderly smoothes her mother's hair.

Lisa closes the door behind us, and I push her gently against it. Before she can say anything, I frame her face with my hands and cover her lips with mine. As I take possession of her mouth, I feel her melt against me as if her body shifts to mold into mine. Her right hand reaches for my waist, and she pulls my shirt out of my pants as if she's desperate for our skin to touch. I slide a knee between her legs, and within seconds, she's riding my thigh. She moans into my mouth, and the sound she makes vibrates all the way to my dick. I'll never get tired of the noises she makes. I let go of her face and slide one hand down the front of her pants. I zero in on the little nub hidden in her wet folds and let her buck against my hand a few times. She catches fire before I have time to slide a finger in her.

She shudders and breaks the kiss to catch her breath. She rests her head on my chest.

"You're good?" I ask.

Her entire body shakes, and I realize she's laughing as if I just asked the funniest question ever.

"Not quite," she says. "I think I still have some room for another desert."

She reverses our positions so that I'm leaning against the door. She fumbles with my belt buckle. My scrambled brain finally registers what she means by desert, and I help reach for it while she drops to her knees in front of me.

I'm not going to last long. I've had fantasies about this, except that in my fantasy, she didn't have one arm in a sling and a bruised shoulder but very available and nimble fingers. I watch her lick her lips and slowly take me into her mouth. Oh fuck... who cares about hands? Her eyes are closed, and when I let out a hiss I see the corner of her mouth rise in a smile. Thank fuck she enjoys doing this because I sure love it. I rest a hand on her head and gently move my hips. I speed up the cadence, and she doesn't balk when I finally burst into her.

She opens her eyes and looks up at me. Turning my question around, she asks, "You're good?"

I help her get to her feet then hold her as tight as I can without hurting her.

"Better than good, baby. Way better than good."

∾

12

She sits on her bed, and I stand in front of her, readjusting my shirt in my pants. I try to think of a nice way to get the touchy subject of her brother's jacket on the table, but I can't. So I just ask, "Where's David's jacket?"

Lisa stiffens as if I had just slapped her. "Why?"

I come closer to the bed and crouch in front of her. "Because I don't think you were the victim of a random attack. I think David must have been onto something, and we may find it hidden somewhere in his jacket."

She thinks about it and shakes her head. "I emptied all the pockets before I started wearing it."

"I'm sure you did, baby, but maybe there was a special pocket you haven't seen. Something in the lining..." I look at her, and she doesn't seem to understand what I want.

I stand up and change my tone from cajoling to authoritative. "Where is it, Lisa?"

She lowers her gaze and answers, "In the left side of the closet."

"Thank you, baby," I say, keeping my voice low.

I open the closet, to find it half-filled with men's clothing, among which I recognize David's jacket. I pull it out of the closet and ask, "Whose clothes are those?"

"Andy's," she answers. "This is his room."

"What do you mean?" My question comes out more aggressively than I would have liked because the idea of her sharing this room with another man is making my temper flare. I lay the jacket on the dresser, to pat it down.

She sighs. "This place belongs to Ten. He's Lyv's husband. Old money, good family. They used to have roommates. There was Xander, Oliver, and Andy... I'll give you the short version. Xander ran away after knocking Lyv up. Oliver—he's a doctor, the one who delivered baby Oliver. He moved out at the end of his residency. The only one that's left is Andy. He's still in and out, depending on the state of his relationship with his girlfriend, and now Ten's moved out, too... I'm praying he'll come to his senses and come back before the baby arrives."

I relax. It's innocent room sharing. They don't really share the room; she uses it while he's away. Still, I'll feel better when she'll be back home.

"If Lyv ever gets tired of running the restaurant, she could come down south with us and run the clubhouse," I say. "She sounds like she's got the collective living thing down pat. In the meantime, I want you to come home as soon as you can."

Lisa laughs, and she comes to stand behind me. "I'm not sure how you're being possessive and bossy makes me feel. Sometimes I like it because it shows me that you care, but sometimes it annoys me because it makes me feel as if you don't trust me."

"I do—fuck, what's that?"

In the shoulder padding of the jacket, I feel a thin square object. I slide my fingers in an opening that looks like it's been done with a razor blade or a sharp knife. I can't catch the object.

Lisa pushes me aside to look and touches the contour of the object with the tip of her fingers. "It's a floppy disk." She trails her finger along the sleeve and finds the opening in the lining. She slides two fingers in it and pulls out a cracked disk.

"Looks like it didn't like being dragged on pavement for a block, either," she says as I gently take it from her. She looks at the disk then at me. Her composure has changed completely. "How did you know?" she asks, her tone accusatory.

"I didn't know. I just took an educated guess. There's nothing special about the jacket, so if someone went all that way to try to take it from you, it means there was something in it."

She gives me a suspicious look while I open my wallet and slide the disk into it, making sure I don't damage the magnetic part.

"Oh, come on, Lisa. Give me a break. Even Lyv realized there had to be something in the jacket to make someone want it, and she's not a detective."

Lisa frowns and seems incredulous. "She did? How do you know?"

"Because she asked me this morning if I was coming over to check it out, and I said yes."

"Oh, I see." Looking very deflated, she takes a step to the door. "I guess now that you have what you came for, you'll be on your way."

The flagrant disappointment in her voice makes me cringe.

"Yeah, I've got to get going, but you know it's not like that," I tell her.

She stops and turns around. I can read the hurt in her eyes.

"Prove it to me," she says, and she holds out her hand. "Just leave the disk with me. I'll make sure it gets to the police. I'm certain they have the right equipment to retrieve whatever data was in there even if it was damaged."

I shake my head. "Nope, not going to happen. I have a tech whiz who will do it, and if I come up with any information that can be useful to the police, I will give it to the only police officer I trust."

"And who might that be?" she asks with a sarcastic tone.

"My brother." I put as much conviction in my voice as I can. I want to convey to her how serious I am about this. "I trust him as much as I trusted your brother." She raises her eyebrows, and I realize she doesn't know who my brother is. Tony never allowed my half brother nor my half sister to visit his house. "Ernest Hatcher is my brother."

"Everest is your brother? He's the other son of the head of the Iron Tornadoes? You're kidding me, right?" I shake my head.

Lisa loses it and starts talking to herself out loud. "Everest was in the task force with my brother? It's like asking the fox to guard the henhouse!" She turns around and glares at me. "Then I guess you're right—something's really wrong with the organization of the police. I will never find out who killed my brother."

"Why do you say that?"

Lisa doesn't seem to hear my question. She rests her head against the door. "I can't believe I was so stupid. Oh, I'm such an idiot…"

Before I have the time to take her in my arms and talk some sense into her, she opens the door and rushes into the main room.

"Brian is leaving," she says to Lyv, who gets up from the sofa and asks, "Is it time to hit the road already?"

"Yes, I have to catch up with the rest of my crew," I tell her. "Thank you very much for a delicious lunch, and I hope that one day, you'll come and visit us in Florida."

Lyv's eyes cloud suddenly, and I can't figure out why, but she smiles and says, "It was lovely meeting you, Brian."

Lisa walks me to the door, and when I bend over to kiss her, she turns her head away and says, "It's fine, Brian. You got what you came for, so there's no need to pretend anymore."

I fight the urge to toss her over my shoulder, bring her back to her room, and show her how crazy I am about her. But I really don't have the time that I need to convince her that she should trust me. I'll wait for both of us to cool down before we can talk this out.

13

A knock on my open door makes me raise my eyes from the incomprehensible invoice from our liquor supplier. I look up, happy for the reprieve. Anything that can distract me from the pile of paper that spontaneously grew on my desk while I was on the road is a welcome relief.

My favorite nerd is standing by the door with a smile on his face. He's the brains behind the Friendly Persuasion Agency. He knows his way around electronic circuits like I know my way around an engine, and if one piece of information can be found in a library or in some administrative document, he's the guy to find it.

"Ice, you got a minute?" he asks.

"Sure thing Whiz. Come on in."

He steps in and delicately closes the door behind him. Watching Whiz move around unsettles me, giving me the impression that the film of my life just went in slow motion. He nonchalantly settles himself in one of the two armchairs on the other side of my desk and opens his messenger bag. He looks into it, and he's so slow that I wonder if he remembers what he's searching for.

I restrain the urge to jump over my desk and toss the contents of his bag on the flat surface to help him remember. But rushing our whiz is counterproductive. He has his own agenda and his own rhythm. If anyone makes him skip a step, he has to restart. Those of us who need his expertise have to slow down and adopt his pace if we want to work with him.

There are only two activities during which Whiz acts like a regular guy: when he rides his bike and when he eats. All his other physical activities are carried out at a leisurely pace, even sex. Well, especially sex. He's objectively nothing to look at, but all the subs of The Styx love him. Talking about foreplay with Whiz brings tears to their eyes. They said deferred gratification takes on a totally new meaning with him, and I absolutely believe it.

But I'm not into delayed anything right now. I dropped the disk at his house this morning, and I just can't wait to find out if he was able to read what was on it. If patience is a virtue, then I have to plead guilty of sin. I'm a very moderately virtuous man.

Whiz finally pulls a transparent plastic storage bag from his bag. He opens it and takes out two colored floppy disks. He closes the bag, leaving the broken one that I had given to him inside.

Unable to wait any longer, I ask, "Did you get what was on it?"

"Some of the data was irretrievable."

I roll my eyes at him. "But you were able to read some of it?"

"Oh, yes, absolutely."

I breathe in deeply and wonder if I should prompt him to continue or if he's going to do it spontaneously. I wait, giving him the benefit of the doubt while he meticulously closes his bag. He looks up at me, and I raise my eyebrows in a silent question.

"All the available documents have been copied on those two disks," he says. "And I also took the liberty of keeping one copy on a hard disk in my home. Obviously, said disk encrypted."

"Obviously," I repeat. My amused tone escapes his notice. Some days, I wonder if he's immune to sarcasm.

"Most of the documents are in ClarisWorks. I printed them." He slowly dives into his bag again and comes back with a bunch of stapled sheets, but this time, he multitasks and talks at the same time. "It's a very nice integrated program for Macs. Anyway, there are a few spreadsheets. I studied them, and I have no doubt it totals some sort of income stemming from various contributors and then computes the distribution of such income. The contributors and beneficiaries are identified by initials, and you can see when payments were made and received. However, by itself, this data is useless since you don't know if this is about tricks turned, grams of coke, or church donations."

Whiz stops, and his gaze gets lost in the distance. Maybe he does that because his mind works so much faster than those belonging to the rest of us, and he feels he needs to give us some time to catch up with his train of thought.

"There is a database that is most interesting and that may help identify the beneficiaries of the payment. It allocates some sections of Florida to some of said beneficiaries. So, for instance, 'MDC' belongs to 'SC' while 'PBC' changed hands about two years ago. It went from 'SW' to 'ST.'"

I immediately think that "SW" could be the initial of Steven Williams, the police captain who married Lisa and David's mother last year, but then I realize I'm jumping the gun because there are probably a dozen other police officers in the county with the same initials.

"What is more interesting," Whiz says, "are the copies of the documents related to various businesses that belong to a corporation called the Unrepentant Southern White Wizards."

"Have you ever heard of them before?"

"Not before this morning, but now, I have found out more than I ever wanted to know about them," Whiz says. "It's the official front of a white supremacist group. If you want their corporate structure and the activities they are involved with, I should be able to gather the data for you within a few days."

"Yeah, please do that."

"Anything in particular I should be looking for?"

"I'm not sure…"

"Maybe if you tell me who the client is, it would help," he suggests.

I think about it for a second and decide to tell him the truth. "I'm the client, and I would appreciate it if you could keep this between us. This is about the murder of a friend of mine. He was a police officer, and he was investigating some local organized crime unit when he was killed."

"That would be Lisa's brother," Whiz says, surprising me once more. Most of the time, he seems oblivious to what's happening around him, but every so often, he says something that proves he's not the absent-minded professor we believe him to be. "I only saw her once, last year when you took her to the clubhouse. She's very lovely. A real sweet girl. You should bring her here someday."

The way he smiles at me, I can't figure out if he's being facetious or not.

Since I have no sense of humor when it comes to Lisa, I snap back at him, "I don't think so."

He laughs. "It figures!" he says, revealing he was baiting me.

Delicately unfolding his long frame from the chair, he tells me that there's a terrified-looking prospect waiting for me at the bar.

That would be Earplugs. Tonight's the night I'm introducing him to Patricia.

≈

14

I ride by my mother's house and see that Tony's car is gone. I park half a block away and return to her house on foot. I walk through the backyard and peek through the kitchen door; Mum's sitting at the table, nursing a cup of coffee, with a novel in hand. When I knock on the glass part of the door, she looks at me and smiles. It's a sad smile, but still, it's a smile.

"Come on in, Brian," she says as she gets up and pours me a cup. "Did you have breakfast? I can cook up something for you."

"No thanks, Mum." A wave of guilt washes over me as she struggles to keep her smile. Feeding her loved ones is her favorite way to show her affection. Turning down breakfast after we just started talking again is a major mistake on my part.

"Can I get a rain check? I worked all night, and I just dropped by to give you a hug on my way to bed," I explain.

She nods. The ghost of David hovers in the kitchen. She did say she believed me when I swore to her that the Iron Tornadoes had nothing to do with his death and that he was not investigating us, but I can still feel the shadow of a doubt lingering. Tony probably keeps it alive.

"What did you do last night?" she asks, breaking the silence.

"Caught up on the paperwork at The Styx and supervised the evening. It was a quiet one."

"That's good, I guess." She twirls her spoon in her coffee.

I gave my mother a watered-down idea of what The Styx is, presenting the sex club as an alternative place to do things that you can't do in your own home for lack of space or privacy. She was puzzled at first, but she got it when I told her about this member who was very vocal during sex and stopped enjoying it when she had to remain silent for fear of waking her kids.

"It makes sense to go to a place where there's a sound-proof room that's a club instead of a cheap motel," she admitted then.

I also explained that the club offers some equipment that some members don't have the space for in their own homes. I even made her laugh when I told her about the Tantra chair a friend of mine had purchased and how, after their sons had adopted the very curvaceous chair as their miniature car race track, he and his wife could not make love on it anymore without giggling like idiots.

Talking about sexual activities with my mother was weird, but somehow, I find it healthier than lying to her about what I do.

"How are the newlyweds?" I ask, trying to find a subject that will be easier on her.

"They're good," she says. "I would never say this to Tony, but I think she's a lot happier with Steven than she was with her first husband."

I nod. David and Lisa's father was Tony's twin brother. He died a long time ago, and I don't remember him that well.

"Of course, now they need to adapt to Lisa moving back in, but I understand it's temporary, only until she passes the bar."

"When is Lisa arriving?" I ask.

"She's been here for a few days," my mother says, and instantly, I'm mad. Mad that she's been back and that I haven't seen her. Given where we were when I last rode away from her, I'm not surprised she didn't come to the clubhouse to let me know she was back.

"I think she looks terrible," my mother adds.

"How so?" I avoid her gaze to hide my feelings.

"Sad, broken. It's like something inside her has been shattered again, but she keeps going. She's registered for this bar preparation intensive seminar. Good thing it's held really close, in the conference center of the Central Hotel. Steven drops her off every morning, and she walks back home. Betty and I offered to drive her back, but she says she needs the fresh air and the exercise."

Good, now I know how I'm going to manage to get some alone time with her.

"Now you, young man, look like you badly need to get some sleep."

"You're right, Mum. It's time I head back home."

The very second I call the clubhouse my home, my mother cringes. As far as she's concerned, this house should still be my home. But that's not what her husband thinks anymore. Tony doesn't want me around since I stopped blindly doing what he wanted me to do.

Tony gave me one, and only one, pass. I used it the day David and I ran away to enlist. So when I decided not to become a cop and went to work with the Iron Tornadoes, well with Cracker, I had no passes left. As far as Tony's concerned, joining the club was nothing more than an act of betrayal. He doesn't get that the motorcycle club is a form of brotherhood that works for me and that Everest and Juliya are my blood and my family.

I hug my mother and return to my bike. Instead of getting back to the clubhouse right away as I initially planned, I ride to the Central Hotel and get the schedule of Lisa's classes. It's easy enough to remember: nine to five every single day of the week. I have enough time to go home and grab a few hours of sleep then catch her as she gets out.

At five fifteen, Lisa's still not out. I lock the bike and enter the hotel lobby. Walking through the main bar, I see Lisa in a booth with two other girls. Each holds a handful of index cards, and they take turns reading from them, probably prepping for the test. I retreat to a spot by the entrance and settle on a tall chair next to the cute barmaid's working station.

"Hello, Ice," she says, flashing me a pretty smile. "Long time, no see."

I rack my brain, trying to figure out where I know her from. Since she called me Ice, it's gotta be MC related.

"Good to see you, angel," I tell her while flipping through my virtual memory cards. I order a beer, and when she comes back with it, I still have no idea who she is.

"You don't remember me, do you?" she says with a coquettish smile.

I laugh and plead guilty. She tilts her head exaggeratedly and twirls in front of me. She's built like a goddess, and her uniform leaves little to the imagination. When I see it, I realize she's not doing this to show of her scrumptious ass. That's an added benefit. She's showing me the tattoo of a blue bird that would otherwise have remained hidden under her jet-black ponytail.

"Birdy!" I say, giving the girl a new look over. She's one of Brains's daughters, one from the first litter, as he would say.

"You're looking good, baby." And I mean it. She's wearing way too much makeup for my taste, but otherwise, she looks good enough to eat.

"You're not looking too bad yourself," she tells me.

"Happy to know you're back in town. How long have you been working here?"

"A couple of weeks. I arrived the day you and my dad left to go babysit a rock star," she tells me. "Landed this job on the first day, and it's really a cool place to work."

A customer at the other end of the bar finishes

nursing his drink and calls her over. She comes back to me with a flier for a special event organized at the hotel.

"I know I'll see you at the Fourth of July barbecue at the clubhouse." She puts the flier down on the bar in front of me. "But before this, we're having a big event on June fifteenth to celebrate the one-year anniversary of the opening of this place. You should come."

Without waiting for my answer, she strolls away from the bar and through the room, collecting orders. She stops at Lisa's table and takes the girls' orders before returning to her station.

"Virgin piña colada and diet sodas," she says, wrinkling her nose. "Those ladies are not getting drunk for a few weeks. They're a bunch of would-be lawyers preparing for the bar exam."

"Yeah, I know," I tell her, grinning. "One of them is my girl."

"Really?" she says. "I didn't know you had an old lady already."

"Well, she's not really my old lady yet, but she will be."

"Lucky girl." Birdy winks at me.

I laugh and tell her, "I'm on her shit list right now, so she'll need a little convincing."

"You could start by putting their drink on your tab," Birdy suggests.

"Good thinking. A man should always have a wise woman like you as his strategy advisor," I tell her while she tallies up my bill. I put some cash on the bar and look at the flier.

The picture looks familiar, but I don't recognize it for

a few seconds. It's the picture on David's postcard, and now I remember Cracker's observation about this tower being a sore thumb in the middle of Point Lookout. That was what had been bugging me all along. It was not a spring break picture; it was the huge party the hotel management threw for the opening on June fifteenth last year. That means the postcard was definitely printed after David's death. So, yeah, Everest got it right—David's not dead!

I get up and rush out of the bar. Talking to Lisa can wait. I need to find Everest and figure out where David is hiding. God help me, I want to kill him for putting Lisa and me through this misery for a year.

~

15

I drive to the police station and park by my brother's bike, where I wait for him to come out. Ever since he's been off the task force, he has regular hours. When he does come out at six, he's not really surprised to see me. Every so often, I drop by the station when I need some information I can't get without the help of the force.

"What do you need?" he asks, dispensing with the civilities.

"I need to know how much you trust your captain."

Obviously hesitant about his answer, he leans against the fence and runs a hand in his short hair. "He had a bad rep when he arrived."

"Bad how?" Bad can mean several things. A corrupt cop is a bad cop, but so is a cop that rats to Internal Affairs or sleeps with his partner's wife.

"I don't know," he explains. "No one would come out and say anything specific. No one's ever accused him of being on the take or alleged that he was a mole for IA. There was just this rumor that he was not to be trusted." Everest stares at the tip of his boots as if they hold the answers to the mysteries of the world. He closes his eyes and goes on. "At some point, I thought it was just some weird sort of superstition because he lost three partners on the job."

"Wow, three partners!" That would make anyone think twice about going out on the street with him.

"Yes, and all gunned down, too," Everest adds. "At one retirement party, I met an older cop who told me that on two out of the three instances, he was with his partner and was badly shot, as well. But somehow, he managed to survive both times."

Since he still hasn't answered my question, I ask, "What does your gut tell you?"

"I think he's clean and working with Internal Affairs," Everest spits out. "I think your pal David was working with them, as well, and they faked his death because something went sour in their investigations."

"I think you're right, and I'd like to have a sit-down with your captain outside of the station. You think you can arrange that?"

"He's still in his office. I'll go back in and ask him."

While I wait for Everest to return, I see Mike coming out of the station. I remember him from the police academy. He was friendly enough, but something about him was off. David thought I was paranoid.

"Hey, Brian," he says, walking toward me and extending his hand. "Long time, no see."

"How's life been treating you?" I ask.

"Been doing good," he says. "I've got a desk job, and I'm loving it. Much safer than all the street action. Soon, we'll be just as bad as Miami."

"What do you mean?" Miami seems like a pretty good place to live to me if you're into big city life.

"Well, ya know, it's the salad bowl thing."

"Now you've lost me," I tell him.

"Oh, come on," he says, sounding exasperated. "Don't tell me you haven't noticed it, too."

I shrug to show I really don't know, so he elaborates.

"In the old days, anyone who came here would start by learning English and adapt to fit in. The English, the Irish, even the Germans and even the Poles—they all managed to adapt. It was the great melting-pot era. Nowadays, no one wants to integrate. The melting pot has been transformed into a big salad bowl. They all wanna keep their cultural identity, so the Haitians go on babbling in Créole while the spics never bother to learn English."

I stare at him and wonder if he's that open on this subject in the station. I'm guessing he's not because it's definitely a diversified working place.

"Don't look at me like that," he says. "It's not like the motorcycle clubs are not selective about who they let in, and I won't ever blame you for being picky and sticking with your own kind."

"You're right," I tell him. "There's some people you clearly don't want to be associated with."

The look in his eyes tells me that the irony of my tone has not been lost on him. He's sharper than I thought.

Probably realizing that he shouldn't have been so

forthright with me, he says good-bye and snaps, "Next time, you shouldn't park here. It's reserved for members of the police force. You lost that right when you dropped out of school."

His choice of words is interesting. I didn't drop out; I resigned, which is totally different, but I think he knows and was trying to be insulting.

A few minutes later, Everest comes out and says that Captain Williams will be expecting us at his house around eight. That gives me enough time to drive by the Friendly Persuasion Agency offices and see if Whiz has made any progress on his investigation about the contents of the disk.

And he has.

"I've drawn a chart for you." He slowly unfolds a few pages taped together like a paper maze or puzzle. "They're worse than a virus spreading throughout Florida. They start by finding a way to get a toe in an activity, and soon, they take over and have everyone marching to their tune."

He starts showing me how the Unrepentant Southern White Wizards have acquired a controlling or decisive interest in a large majority of the gun stores in the area and how they have now directed their interest in strip joints.

"That's the only activity for which the USWW Corp seems color-blind," he says.

"What do you mean?"

"All their other business are run by Caucasians and cater exclusively to them. The pussy trade, however, is more diversified. They're all over the map, and even if the management stays white, the talent is more diverse."

"Thank you, Whiz. You've done amazing work," I tell him. "Can I take the chart with me? I would like to show it to someone tonight."

"Sure, this is for you. I've got it all in my head," he says while meticulously refolding his paper creation. "Now that I've done that with the corporate structures, I'm looking at the people behind them. If you give me another week, I should be able to provide you with some interesting information. But I can tell you right now, some of those places are owned outright by a few politicians or high-ranking police officers."

"How is this possible?" I ask. "With all the dirt the politicians throw at each other during an election, I'm surprised their political opponents didn't out them about any sort of borderline activity."

"Someone tried with Ervaners," he reminds me. "He owns a few buildings in a shopping center. One of them was initially a bar and grill, then a bar, and then it became a strip joint. Don't you remember? When put on the spot, he explained that the way the twelve-year lease had been written, the tenant's lawyer was allowed to modify the activity carried out on the premises and that his hands were tied."

I nod and take the chart he hands to me.

"He's not getting re-elected," he says.

"Is that so?"

"Yeah," Whiz says with a malicious grin. "He got a taste of his own medicine. Do you remember how he used the municipal police to get his town sanitized after being elected?" He exaggerates his southern accent as he pronounces the word sanitized, and I nod to show that I understand what type of sanitation he's talking about.

"They used the most absurd reasons to stop and search selected targets and then hold them until immigration came to check their status. When they found illegal aliens, they took them away. As a consequence, anyone with a questionable status fled the town, and today, the 'good people' of his town are complaining about the increase in the cost of labor. Funny how people with no fear of being deported have the gall to require minimum wage."

The way Whiz presents the situation surprises me, making me smile. It shouldn't because politically, the only thing he believes in is karma.

I'm not so optimistic. I'm not certain that what goes around always comes around. I've seen too many people get away with murder.

16

I t's five to eight when I park my bike in front of Lisa's house. Doing so is kind of weird because during the last year, I've made a habit of parking a block away when I come visit either my mother or Lisa. I look over at the other side of the lawn, to the identical construction in which my mother and Tony live. I can't see if anyone's home.

At Lisa's house, which is now the captain's home too, the garage door is open, and the space is empty, except for David's cross-country bike in the far corner. It looks all greased up and ready to go. I wonder if Lisa's been riding it again.

Everest's Harley is next to Captain Williams's truck in the driveway. Both men are sitting on the porch swing, taking up the entire seat of what is supposed to be a three-seater. Williams drops his cigarette in his can of beer and crushes it as he gets up.

We shake hands and gauge each other for a few

seconds. Our paths have crossed several times, but we've never officially met before.

"Nice to meet you," I say as I decide that I was right to trust Everest's gut feeling about the man. I like the firmness of his handshake and the way his gaze meets mine. It doesn't waver, as if he has nothing to hide and no preconceived ideas about me.

"Same here," he says. "Let's get started while the girls are out."

"He sent them to the movies," Everest explains.

That's good thinking; it would have been kind of weird otherwise.

As we enter, I notice a few changes in the familiar house. The captain has been taking really good care of the place. The decor hasn't changed much, but there's been a fresh coat of paint and this lived-in look. Not looking like a perfect showroom or model house, as it did when Lisa's mother was single, makes the place more pleasant.

Steven Williams brings a six-pack of beer and some tacos from the kitchen and gets straight to the point while we sit around the dining room table.

"Everest here says that you believe David's still alive. Can you tell me why?"

"I know for a fact it's not his body in the coffin you put in the ground last spring," I say, avoiding part of his question.

"But you don't want to tell us how?" The captain asks.

"Let's just say that David reached out to me."

"I thought you had a good explanation for the post-card," Everest says.

"I did until I realized that the card was printed in June of last year, weeks after he was supposedly dead."

"That boy is an idiot," Steven Williams snaps.

"So you knew?" Everest asks.

"Yeah, he and I work for Internal Affairs. We are part of a special unit investigating the infiltration of our rank by some Aryan group."

"You mean the Unrepentant Southern White Wizards?" I ask.

Steven Williams's head snaps to look in my direction as he asks, "What do you know about them?"

I hesitate for a second before I decide to go all in and show him my entire hand. From the inside pocket of my jacket, I pull out the plastic bag with the broken disk as well as Whiz's chart and start spreading it out on the table.

Ignoring the disk, Captain Williams takes his glasses out of his shirt pocket and studies the chart. With his fingers, he follows the arrows that lead from one corporation to another, showing how the network is interconnected.

"This is excellent work," he says. "Our guys have a few you didn't catch, but you have several that have escaped us so far."

Everest studies the chart silently then asks, "What got you started in that direction?"

"The information collected on this disk that I found in David's leather jacket," I say.

"Come again," Steven Williams says. "I checked the pockets of that jacket before Lisa took it with her to New York, and there was nothing in them."

"It was in the shoulder padding." I tell him about the Aryans trying to get David's jacket from Lisa.

"Is that how she got hurt?" the captain asks. "She told her mother she got shot by a crazy guy during a Xander Wild concert."

"That was a separate incident."

"She sure has been riding a rough patch," Everest notices.

"Yeah, that's for sure," Williams says. "But then, so did her brother. He started working on one of the girls who was working in a strip joint operated by the Wizards. Jeanne-Michelle was a sweet girl from Haiti who started feeding us information after David told her what kind of people her bosses were. Even though he never came clean with it, I'm pretty sure she and David had a thing going. Can't blame the kid. She was lovely and a drop-dead beauty." He shrugs and cracks open one of the cans before continuing with the story.

"A few days before David's official death, he left his favorite jacket to dry at Jeanne-Michelle's place after being caught under a torrential rain. When he came to retrieve it the next day, the place had been thoroughly tossed, mattress ripped apart and all, and the woman had vanished. Since everyone knew he had a sweet spot for that girl, he felt comfortable enough to ask the other strippers about her and found out that her locker had been emptied by the management the very day she had vanished. And they weren't really looking for her."

"So you guys figured out she had stolen something from them and either ran away or been killed before she had a chance to hand it over to David while, all along, David had the disk hidden in his jacket," I say.

"Right, but then the management started questioning all Jeanne-Michelle's Johns, and somehow, David's cover got blown. That's when we knew we had to pull him out and, to avoid retaliation against his family, stage his death," Captain Williams says.

"Did you ever find out who blew his cover?" I ask.

"It has to be someone from our station," he says. "David joined us right out of the police academy, so he was not a familiar face to anyone but us."

"It could be the same person who had been feeding Lisa false information," Everest adds. He answers the question he must read in my raised eyebrows. "Last year, she asked me when we were going to clear the streets of the Iron Tornadoes. I figure someone must have told her that it was our MC her brother was investigating, right?"

"The only person Lisa's been friendly with at the station, as far as I know, is Mike," Williams volunteers. "He was the one on reception duty when she came to get her brother's stuff and then again when she dropped by afterwards."

"He fits the profile," I say.

"I'm not sure," Williams says. He furrows his brows and stares into the distance as if he's flipping mental images of the guy. "I don't think I ever saw him befriend anyone in the station. He's polite and amicable but never volunteers any personal information. If I didn't have access to his personnel file, I wouldn't be able to tell you if he's single or where he lives. He did belong to some right-wing association when he was in high school, but it wasn't held against him when he filed. Boys will be boys. We all did stupid things when our hormones were overriding our brains."

His admission puzzles me since he seems like the type of guy who has always had everything under control. Maybe not. Could he have done some crazy shit in his days, too? I try to visualize him in a hippy commune, smoking grass or dropping acid, but my imagination's not powerful enough to conjure such images.

"Mike did suggest to a young recruit that there was a way to stop and search people without serious probable cause, because if you waited long enough, you could get them for jaywalking," Williams adds.

"But there's no jaywalking laws in Florida," Everest interjects.

"Almost none," I say. "The law does prohibit pedestrians from crossing between adjacent intersections where traffic control signals are in operation. So you see, if there are two traffic signals—which is the case when you're in Point Lookout or most other cities—you can actually stop someone for a traffic stop violation if they step out of line."

Captain Williams looks at me as if I've grown a second head. "That's precisely what Mike told the recruit."

"We were taught that at the police academy by one very conservative criminal law teacher who thought civil rights were nothing more than encumbrances thrown in our way by 'bleeding heart and soft judges,' who, according to him, should have been sentenced to walk some wild beat for a week to live with their decisions."

Williams laughs. "I know precisely who you're talking about. He's lost his teaching position this year. He was doing too much damage."

"So where's David?" I ask.

"I don't know. This is information given on a need-to-know basis, and I don't need to know. But you should see him soon enough," Captain Williams says. "We're doing a three-state coordinated action on Monday morning under the supervision of the Feds." He pronounces supervision as if the word left a bad taste in his mouth. "After that, he should be free to come home."

"And you're gonna be in so much trouble, man. I really feel for you!"

Looking genuinely surprised, Captain Williams looks at me while a big grin spreads across Everest's face. Everest gets it. Captain Williams will have to tell his wife that he's slept by her side for almost a year without telling her that the son she was mourning wasn't really dead.

"You're gonna have to tell Betty," I tell him.

He cringes. "Right." He huffs and throws his hands up in the air. "I know. I figure I'll wait 'til the last minute, take the most sheepish look I can muster, and then pray she'll be so happy to see him that she'll forget about being mad at me." He levels a look at me. "And what about you? Are you looking forward to telling Lisa?"

"You're leaving it up to me? That's fine. No sweat. Hey, I just found out today. It's not as if I had been hiding it from her for a year! Furthermore, I'm on her shit-list right now, and I think that may earn me some points to get back in her good graces."

"You mean in her pants," Everest says with a wink.

"That, too," I admit.

"I guess that will make us family then," Captain Williams says. "You should start calling me Steven."

"Fine. I will, but tell me something, Steven. Do you have any idea how they found out about Lisa having the jacket and being in New York?"

"Lisa in New York—that's easy. Betty is so proud of her daughter going to the big city to study law that she has chewed more ears about it than I care to count. So the question would really be who has managed not to hear about Lisa being in New York. But the jacket... I don't know."

"Talk of the devil," Everest says. "Here they come."

17

I brace myself for impact as Betty and Lisa walk into the room. Betty takes in the three of us sitting at her dining room table and shrugs, staring at her husband.

Lisa asks, to no one in particular, "What are those two doing here?"

Betty puts a calming hand on her daughter's shoulder and tells her husband, "Steve, next time you want us out because you need privacy, just tell me. That way, I know not to come back home too early." She sighs. "But since we're here, I think Lisa has a valid question. Boys, what are you doing here?"

I stand up and take a step in the direction of the two women while I hear the sound of Everest fighting with the pages of Whiz's chart, trying to fold them up without tearing them apart.

Lisa stands in front of Betty as if to protect her from me.

"Hello, Aunt Betty," I say, ignoring Lisa's angry glare. "It's good to see you again."

"Hello, Brian," she says, her voice choked with emotion. Pushing her daughter aside, she takes a few steps in my direction then stands on her tiptoes and takes my face in her hands. Tears shine in her eyes as she tells me, "I've missed you so much. As if it wasn't bad enough to lose David, you had to go and break my heart, too, by staying away." I lift her in my arms and hug her.

"I'm sorry," I say. "I shouldn't have let my dispute with Tony get in the way. I should have been here for you."

Feeling her tears against my shirt as she holds on to me, I turn toward Steve and silently ask him for permission to tell her now.

He looks torn. He obviously would love to put an end to her misery, but he's sworn to secrecy, and he won't break down.

"Oh, enough with all that drama," Everest says. "Steven, for God's sake, you trusted her enough to marry her."

"What are hiding from us?" Lisa asks.

"If you come with me, I'll show you," I say, letting Betty go as her husband reaches out for her.

Lisa looks at Everest and Steven. Both nod to her then her mother.

"Go clear the air with him," Betty says. "I never believed the rumor that his club had anything to do with David's death."

"Thank you," I say. "It's nice to know I had your trust."

As I start toward the door, I realize Lisa's not moving. I take a few steps back and catch her hand. "Come on, sweet butt. It's time for a ride."

From the corner of my eye, I see Steven grinning and Everest rolling his eyes at me as if to tell me that I should know better. I do, but I so love teasing her, I can't help myself.

She sits on my bike while I go into her open garage to grab a helmet for her. After she puts it on, she sits up straight with both hands on the back rest. We played this game before—last year, when we were leaving the spring rock festival, where I found her with Everest and his pals while the Friendly Persuasion team was working security.

I start the bike and purposely hit every pothole in the street until she relents and puts her arms around my waist. I rest one hand on hers, but it's not enough for her to relax this time.

I take her past the clubhouse, to my piece of land. I park the bike at the entrance of the clearing and pull my backpack out of my saddlebag. Taking her hand, I make her walk to the center of the small hill where I want our house to be built. I unfold the blanket from my bag and motion for her to sit facing the water.

The shining moon reflects in the small pond on the other side of the clearing. I couldn't have ordered a more perfect setting.

"Why did you bring me here, Brian?" she asks with both hands fisted on her hips. She puts up a brave front, but I know that when I tell her about her brother, all that sharp polish is going to crack.

"Because this will be your home soon," I say. "I

purchased the land for us a while back, and I've been waiting for you to come back to begin construction. You need to pick the layout and shit…" Nothing came out the way I wanted.

"You're out of your mind," she hisses through her teeth. "Whatever made you think that I'm going to move here, in the middle of nowhere, and furthermore, with you?"

I put one hand on the small of her back and another on her neck. "The way you shudder every single time I touch you. The way you look at me. The fact that when you stop trying to convince yourself that you hate me, you know that you're in love with me."

She looks away from me and searches for something to say deep inside the pond. Before she finds inspiration, I add, "Also, I have two things to tell you that are going to make you a bit crazy, and if you're going to scream, right here seems like the ideal place to do it."

She looks back at me. Her head is tilted, and lips, parted. It's an invitation I can't resist. I take her mouth, and her hands leave her hips. She grabs a fistful of my shirt and tangles her other hand in my hair. I apply a little pressure to her back, and she molds into me. When she does that, I have no doubt that she's my other half. She's the one I need to be complete.

I let go of her mouth to nibble on her neck and lose myself in the nest of her breasts. Then I realize I have all but forgotten what I was about to tell her. I pull away for a few seconds, long enough to bring her down to the ground with me.

"Brian," she whispers as I gently trail my mouth along

her collarbone. "Is that how you plan to make me scream?"

"Yes and no. There's something I need to tell you, but I'm not sure I should tell you now or after I make love to you here."

"Will it make me happy or sad?" she asks.

"Happy. Definitely happy." I suspect my smile is so large that I'm wearing an ear-to-ear grin.

"Love me first," she says. "I've missed you so much."

"You're not mad at me anymore?" I whisper into her neck. I can never get enough of that soft spot right at the beginning of her shoulder.

"No," she answers with a breathy voice. "I realized I was being unfair to you when I saw the disk on the table. You're really trying to find who killed David."

I can't delay telling her anymore. If I do, she'll be mad at me all over again, and no matter how much I like makeup sex, I hate drama. So I tell her, "The thing is, baby, he's not dead."

"What!" That comes out just as loud as I'd expected it would, and I'm glad we're in the middle of nowhere.

"His death was all staged by Internal Affairs," I explain.

"When did you find out?" she asks.

"Today." I'm telling the truth, but I see no use in volunteering that I've suspected for a while. Otherwise, she would tear me apart for not telling her sooner.

"And what about Captain Fantastic?" she asks. "Has he known all along?"

There's never enough male solidarity when it comes to

fighting women's wrath, so I just say, "I'm not sure when he found out."

"My mother's going to kill him," Lisa says with a strange voice. I pull away to look at her face and realize she's laughing and crying at the same time. I wipe away her tears with my thumbs, just as she did with mine ages ago, when I thought her brother had died.

"Steven or David?" I ask.

"Both, I think."

"I'll help her with David. The bastard waited way too long to let me know he was alive. But enough talking about those guys. I want you to concentrate on me and only me now." I unbutton her jeans and slide a hand under her shirt.

"Make me," she says.

"Oh, baby girl, you're going to have to learn not to provoke me like that or be ready to deal with the consequences." I pull down her pants and settle myself between her legs.

"Somehow, I think I'm going to love your retaliation." I can hear the smile in her voice, and I know she trusts me entirely.

"Will you play games with me?" I ask, trailing kisses and bites along the inside of her thighs.

"What kind of games?" Her voice is a murmur.

"Naughty games, of course." I stop talking because I'm making a feast out of her. I love everything about her. Her smell, her taste, and the way she arches under my caresses. I love the way she pants and moans and the way she says my name when I make love to her. I love the way she pulls my hair to try to get me to stop, saying it's too much while her hips tilt to increase the pressure of my mouth on her.

Only when I feel her shatter under my caress do I climb up along her body. "Can I come in with no protection?" I ask, looking at her lovely face in the moonlight.

She tilts her head and says, "No birth control." There's a little edge in her voice as she says it, as if she's leaving it up to me. She has no idea what this much trust does to me. I bury myself in her, thinking it would just be perfect if we got a family started on the very site we're going to build our home.

18

The grounds around the clubhouse are full. The air smells like beer, barbecue, and cotton candy. It smells like Independence Day. It smells like happiness.

I've always had a fondness for that day, because whether I spent it with my mother or here at the clubhouse with my father, I was allowed to run wild and free for an entire day while the adults were too busy partying to offer any real supervision.

Today is even more special because, for the first time, I won't have to pick between two families. Today, I'm celebrating with Everest and Juliya as well as Lisa. Everest and Lisa even talked Betty and Steven into coming around for a drink. Getting a police captain to attend an MC's annual bash will no doubt be interesting. Lisa's also been pleading my case with Tony. She thinks I don't know, but I've noticed the conspiratorial looks she's been exchanging with my mother.

The fact that David's not dead has somehow mellowed Tony, and I'm hoping he'll come around and become civilized with me again. But his coming to an MC bash—that would really surprise me. Still, what better way to find out for himself what this whole community is all about?

Lisa is with Juliya, tossing the salads next to the main table.

I have this stupid grin on my face because she's wearing the cut I gave her. The patch on the back proclaims that she's my property. She's given me the whole lecture about slavery being abolished and said that there's no way in hell she will ever consider herself my property. Still, she took it, and she's wearing it proudly.

"Today, the cut, tomorrow the ring... who's gonna wear the collar?" Sledge asks.

He's the main dungeon master at The Styx, and he pretends not to understand that some of us like an equal partnership with our lovers outside the bedroom. I punch him playfully, and he laughs.

"You're so pussy whipped," he says. "Just as bad as Earplug."

I look in the direction he's pointing, and I see Daniel —now officially Earplugs—walking around, two steps behind Patricia looking at her adoringly.

Sledge sights and adds, "Soon, she'll prevent you from going to work and doing your job. You need to take her there and show her who's the boss."

"Not going to happen," I say. "You can tease all you want. I'm not bringing her there or sharing her with anybody."

"The guys are right—you've got it bad. Does she even know why you're called Ice?" he asks.

"No I don't," Lisa says, coming up behind Sledge. "Every time I ask, he distracts me, and I forget."

I wrap a protective arm around Lisa because Sledge is a lady-killer. On a Greek god's body, he wears an angelic smile, but he's the devil. I can't have my woman flying too close to him.

"It's not something he can tell," Sledge explains. "It's something that he has to demonstrate. It's all about the cold burn. That's his specialty, and it's highly addictive."

Lisa looks at me then turns to look back at Sledge, who has vanished.

"So now that your friend has teased me, I have to ask again. Why Ice?"

"But he just told you, sweetheart. It's because of the cold burn." I know very well that I'm doing nothing more than piquing her curiosity.

"What's the 'cold burn'?"

"We could sneak away to my room, and I could demonstrate right away, or you could wait until after dinner. It all depends on how much anticipation you like."

I can see she's intrigued, but before she has the time to decide, Everest joins us.

"Hey, bro, you'll never believe who just arrived," he says.

We turn around to find Steven and Betty, followed by Tony and my mother. Tony looks about as comfortable as a nun in a sex club, and Betty is wearing her deer-in-the-headlight look.

"Don't worry. It's going to be fine," I tell Lisa. "Today is a family-type party. Nothing wild will happen before the kids have been sent home. By then, our parents should all be gone."

We hug, and I introduce Everest and Juliya to Tony. Cracker walks by, and there's a very awkward moment when he hugs my mother.

"Still looking good, Cupcake," he tells her, using the nickname she had when she was living with the club more than thirty years ago. His long-term memory is still intact.

He turns to Tony and extends his hand. I'm flabbergasted when Tony takes it. Force of habit will make people do strange things. Tony's not a man to insult another by refusing a good shake.

"Thank you for raising my boy," Cracker says. "You did a damn good job of it."

"It was my pleasure," Tony says.

They're both acting so civilized, it's getting way too mushy for me. Tony, I get. My mother and Lisa read him the riot act, but Cracker... the disease must really be eating away Cracker's brain cells. But then I notice the smile on Juliya's face. If anybody could talk Cracker into being so polite, it has to be her. Too bad her mother refused to attend the party because I'm sure Juliya would have made her proud.

Cracker takes my kid sister by the arm and leads her away to the barbecue, and the rest of my weird family follows.

"So about this cold burn," Lisa says with a naughty smile I love.

"Anything for the satisfaction of my lady," I tell her.

We discreetly leave the group to enter the clubhouse and climb up to my room. I close the hurricane shutters and dim the lights. We both remove our clothes, and just looking at her, I know she's anxious and excited at the same time.

"This is about the games I like to play," I tell her.

An enthusiastic glimmer flashes in her eyes.

"You need to trust me."

"You know I do." She looks at me with so much love in her eyes that I almost forget to breathe.

I lay her on my bed and get a red silk rope out of the dresser drawer. It's brand-new; I purchased it just for her. Red is her color. It shows off her pale skin. Her eyes widen when I tie it around her wrist and to the hidden hook of the headboard of my bed. I'm not tying her feet today because I need to ease her into this. She doesn't protest when I wrap the red silk scarf around her eyes.

She just whispers, "Be gentle, my love."

"With you, always." I take out my own secret mixture of peppermint oil from my bedside drawer and settle myself comfortably next to her. I bring the tiny bottle under her nose, and she inhales the sent.

"Breathe it in. Yes, good. Again... do you know that peppermint is an aphrodisiac?" I continue without waiting for her answer. "The smell goes straight to your brain. It stimulates the sexual arousal zones so, yes, I want you to breathe it in one more time."

She turns her head toward me and asks for a kiss... I brush her lips with mine, and she protests. I linger a little more, and I can't help but smile.

This is a woman who promised she would never beg.

When I see how mellow just the scent of the oil is making her, I can't wait to see how she will react when it works its magic on her skin.

"But that's not all this wonderful oil does," I say, letting a few drops of the oil fall onto her breasts. "When it touches the skin, the first thing you feel is a cooling sensation, but then…"

The expression on her face changes as I massage her and the initial cold magically turns into an incredible warmth. What I feel in the palm of my hand is nothing compared to what it does to her delicate skin.

"Do you feel the heat, my sweet?" I don't need her to answer me to know that she does.

After a few more drops around her navel, I know she's starting to burn. I close the bottle and set it aside before I kneel between her legs. In a few seconds, the touch of my hand will set her on fire.

When the essence soaked into the skin of my finger comes in contact with the even finer skin of her delicate fold, her breath catches.

"Oh, Brian, it's incredible," she says. "It's cold, and yet I feel so warm."

My caresses bring fuel to her fire, and I watch with delight as her hips rise from the mattress. I want to bury myself into her and put out the fire, but I don't. No matter how much I want to, I won't until she surrenders.

Her body rises and falls as she tries to buck against my hand and gets so close to the edge. I'm so hard, I negotiate her release with myself. Maybe she doesn't have to beg this time. Maybe it will be enough if she just asks…

And she does.

Her fingers wrapped around the red velvet cord, her luscious body arched on the bed, she calls out for me, "Brian, please…"

That's all I wanted—that's all I need from her.

"Oh, baby," I answer. "I was waiting for you. I thought you'd never ask."

As I enter her and share the cold burn with her, I whisper in her ear. "You're mine, you know. Mine forever. I will never let you go."

I hope you've enjoyed Lisa and Ice's story.

Did you know that if you only leave a star rating on your device, I will never know if you liked the story or not?

The only way I can learn what my readers liked is if I see it reviewed. It only takes two words to make an author's day or inspire us in the middle of the night when we can't sleep searching for a new twist in our next novel.

I am most grateful to those who take a minute to post a positive thought that will encourage others to pick up a copy.

ALSO BY OLIVIA

Artistic License

The Wrong Side of the Law

Play with The Curve Masters

As He Bids

Lost and Found

Found and Kept

Kept and Shared

Keeping Tab

See what's cooking in Paris

Learning Curves (in KU)

Other books

Ripped

Jade (in KU)

ALSO BY OLIVIA - BIKERS

The Iron Tornadoes MC Romance Series

Stone Cold - Available in Audio book

Cold Burn - Available in Audio book

Cold Fusion - Available in Audio book

Cold (Books 1 to 3) Only available in Audio book

Hot Pursuit

Hot Mess

White Hot

Bumpy Ride

Tornado Warning

Storm Advisory

Hurricane Watch (Coming in 2019)

The Category 5 Knights MC Romance Series

Chaser

Saving Belle

ALSO BY OLIVIA & OTHER AUTHORS

with Ava Catori - Flirting with Curves
3 stand alone novels in the same world.
Flirting with Disaster
Flirting with Deception
Flirting with Danger
Flirting with Curves (Bundle)

with Shannon Macallan
Home Bound
Hold Fast

ABOUT THE AUTHOR

Olivia Rigal is a six-time USA Today bestselling author of romantic suspense who joined the Indie publishing movement in 2013 and became a Montlake author in 2018.

A native New Yorker who now splits her time between Florida and France, Olivia brings a rich personal background to her stories that spans everything from being a licensed attorney in New York and Paris, to extensive traveling throughout Southeast Asia, to working in a Paris recording studio and the Clignancourt Flea Market, to being an admin at a world famous auction house in Manhattan, and, yes, as a dog groomer.

These experiences come together in Olivia's romantic suspense novels. While most of the stories she tells are stand alone, beloved characters weave in and out, welcoming readers again and again.

To find out about her latest release or apply to her ARC list you can join her VIP reader's group : https://oliviarigal.com/VIP_BM_E

When she's not writing (or doing that attorney thing), she loves to hang out and chat with readers, usually on Facebook. You can follow her :

-                    On   Instagram https://www.instagram.com/oliviarigal/

- On facebook https://www.facebook.com/AuthorOliviaRigal/

- On amazon https://www.amazon.com/Olivia-Rigal/e/B00EUVOKHO

- On twitter @byoliviarigal

- On Pinterest https://www.pinterest.fr/oliviarigal

- On bookbub https://www.bookbub.com/authors/olivia-rigal

This book is a work of fiction. Even if some locations depicted do exist, the story and event described are totally fictitious. The names, the characters, and the events described have been imagined by the author. Any resemblance with reality would be a coincidence.

28835864R00072

Made in the USA
Lexington, KY
22 January 2019